Holroyd's Folly

By

Peter King

Holroyd's Folly

Prologue.

Jeanne-Michelle Desforestier, known as Mickie to her friends and colleagues, considered breakfast an unfortunate affair that occasionally happens to everyone. She and her roommate, Julie, were sullen over a quarrel the night before, even though the cause of the disagreement was, in her view, at least, nothing to keep over to the following day. Since Julie had a different opinion, she had left the apartment before breakfast.

Left to her own devices, Mickie turned on the coffee machine, but it refused to function, and she debated whether to make tea or settle for orange juice. To add to her frustration, there were no eggs in the refrigerator, her favourite pot of cherry jam was empty, and she had to settle for a peach concoction she usually tried to avoid. When the toaster popped, the bread was burned. This was far from the cheery morning feast that cereal advertisers expect every family to enjoy. She stood up to get more toast and noted with annoyance that she'd spilled some jam on her skirt and had to change.

Returning to the table, the tea was cold, and the toast had assumed that peculiar feel of damp leather, which not even the jam could disguise. Disgruntled, she glanced at the clock on the wall and concluded she had to leave but first to change to jeans and drop the skirt off at the cleaners on the way. *Why am I in a hurry? All I'll do is report more births, marriages, and deaths. If I'm lucky, there'll be a distraction like a pompous official opening of an art fair or a cooking competition. Oh well, another day, another dollar.*

Walking out the door, she stopped to look at herself in the hallway mirror. At 35, she stood well over 5'7" but was beginning to show a little more weight than she would have wished. Her hair showed no hint of grey, and the black skin of her face framed red lips behind which lay startling white teeth. Anyone looking casually at her, would get an impression of motherliness and care, supported by willpower and resolve. *You've come a long way, girl, since you left Haiti. I wish my parents could see me now.*

She glanced over at a fading framed snapshot of her family taken before Papa Doc's Tonton Macoutes came and dragged her father off, never to be seen again. Her mother had died soon after, leaving her to the care of relatives who resented the extra mouth and arranged to get rid of her as quickly as possible. It had not been a pleasant experience, and she did her best to forget it. She vowed to try to make for herself a career in which her parents would be proud.

Just then, the phone rang. She debated whether to ignore it but decided to answer it.

"Mickie, get down here as quick as you can. I have an investigative assignment for you. The owner gave me an urgent request, and I'm thinking of giving it to you," her editor said.

"What's it about?"

"You're probably aware of the illicit drugs coming here, mostly from Mexico?" asked the editor. "The owner thinks it's a worthwhile topic to write about."

"But I know nothing about that, and besides, I've never had an investigative assignment. I wouldn't know where to begin," Mickie replied.

"Well, let's see," replied the editor. "Just get down here as fast as you can so I can brief you."

Chapter 1

Peter Holroyd, Professor of Ming, and Qing Chinese maritime voyages no longer had the enthusiasm of his younger years that had supported his research. He was now happily settled down and near retirement. Much of his energy was spent in going over his files to decide what could be scrapped and what might be worth archiving.

Anyone looking at Professor Peter Holroyd would see a middle-aged man with a wrinkled face and a body inclined to paunchiness. He still preferred to wear an open-necked cotton shirt that had seen better days and now hinted at a frayed collar, while his tweed jacket sported old-fashioned leather patches at the elbows. Professor Peter Holroyd was most definitely out of tune in these days of designer T-shirts, jeans, and hoodies.

Holroyd enjoyed the familiar coziness of his untidy home. Overflowing bookshelves stood against one wall, and carpets and scattered rugs in clashing hues and different patterns covered the floor. He still preferred the company of books to most people. He hated social occasions with their meaningless exchanges of small talk, family news, and tales of holidays in ghastly tourist traps or wildernesses best left to Mother Nature.

He opened the top drawer of his filing cabinet and surveyed its contents. It was full of the academic papers he had written or had used in his search for proof in support of Gavin Menzies's claim that Zheng He, the Ming Dynasty Admiral, had been the first to discover America some 50 years before Columbus. *A lot of wasted energy that was.* In recent years, further discoveries revealed that Menzies was wrong in claiming the Chinese were the first to discover America but might have been correct in claiming the Chinese visited the Americas before Columbus.

The next object in the drawer was a folder with no label. Opening the folder, he found it full of newspaper clippings, the first of which was a report of an award ceremony at which his son received a trophy for a science competition. The next one was of another of his son's award ceremonies.

Holroyd was distracted from his original intent and settled back to examine the content, revisit past events, and whatever else was in the folder. He opened the next item to see it was from a magazine and was headed 'Ming Dynasty coin discovered in Molossia.' *Where and what is Molossia?* He went to his computer and Googled the word.

He read that Molossia, a self-proclaimed micronation near Dayton, Nevada, has received no recognition from any other nation and pays taxes to the local state government. *Why on earth did I keep this idiocy?* He returned to the article and then noted references that might have been the reason to keep it.

He had annotated as worth following up a report by a Buddhist missionary Hoei-Shin, who in 499

AD returned from a long voyage of 20,000 Chinese miles to the East where he had met strange people in a strange land. If correct, he might have reached the west coast of North America, maybe even Mexico.

A Sung Dynasty report dated 1178 that sailors reached a region they called 'Mu-Lan-Pi' that some have since claimed to be a part of what is now California. Also in California, a considerable amount of Chinese porcelain has been found at Drake's Bay, north of San Francisco, and the possible discovery of a medieval Chinese-style junk buried under a sandbank in the Sacramento River near Chico.

In Glenn, California, two farmers hand-boring a well said they found some bronze artifacts that someone, somehow, authenticated as Chinese armour, and two local men used a magnetometer to show the presence of something shaped as an 85-foot-long ship with its bow pointed upstream. Subsequent drilling turned up pieces of metal, nails, and wood fragments which have been carbon-dated to 1410 and identified as cut from Keteleeria, a Chinese evergreen tree unknown in America.

Also near Chico, California, the Gallinomero language spoken by Concow people is similar to Chinese. The Concow people may have been descendants of Chinese sailors. They are noted to have celebrated the same festivals of burning paper as the Chinese.

On the eastern side of San Francisco Bay, stone walls may have been built up and down the hills behind the East Bay, going from San Jose all the way to the Carquinez Straits and continuing north over Sonoma Mountain up through the wine country. The walls form neither animal pens nor appear fort-like, but they resemble a miniature version of the Great Wall of China.

At the time, he dismissed the relevance to his work, but thought it might be worth following up at a later stage. Now, he extracted the article and, putting it next to his computer, continued to read the other articles that referred to his son before replacing them in the folder and putting them on one side to later show it to the family.

Next, he opened a file and found an old email that the Vatican had sent him with a sketch of a column somewhere near Acapulco[1]. At the time, it reminded him of the *Yongning* Temple stele erected near the Amur River and he had surmised the object in Mexico could be a Chinese stele. He also thought he recognized the name of Zhou Man[2] among the carved characters.

He felt a sudden rush of excitement. *The stele might be related in some way to what I read in the Molossia clipping. I wonder if the Molossia article is factual about the finds.*

---

[1] In *Gold Among the Trees*

[2] One of the Ming Dynasty Admirals who participated in exploration voyages under Zheng He.

He found there was scholarly support for the Sung document that the report referred to the west coast of the Americas. Scholarly debate about which country was described by the Buddhist missionary Hui Shen (or Hoei-Shin) included the possibility that the west coast of America, possibly Mexico, was described. The Chinese-style junk buried under the Sacramento River and the ceramics carried by a ship sunk in Bodega Bay probably come from a later period about 300 years ago.

Further support for early Chinese visits may have been discovered by John A. Ruskamp Jr., Ed.D., who reported spotting petroglyphs in Albuquerque's Petroglyph National Monument likely inscribed by a group of Chinese explorers using a script in use during a transitional period of writing in China, not long after 1046 B.C.

Holroyd further found possible but inconclusive support and sat back to consider what he had found. *I have enough clues to warrant a closer look at the stele. I have time on my hands so why not go down and look?*

If I'm correct, the above-noted finds and a Chinese stele built during the Yongle Emperor's reign near the modern Acapulco would finally prove the Chinese, perhaps even Zhou Man, came to the Americas before the Europeans. If I can prove my theories right I can retire satisfied that my searches have not been in vain.

For too long, I have been the subject of doubt and even hostility over my research, but this could turn everything around. I'll have the satisfaction of proving my detractors wrong, be vindicated, and retire in a blaze of glory!

He decided *I'm going to find out.*

No sooner had the decision crossed his mind than he remembered his wife's negative reaction when he had previously suggested a visit. *I wonder if she would agree now.* But then he reflected, *Things are going quite well, and I'd be foolish to even think of another foray supporting a quest long past its shelf life.*

He had met his wife, Pearl, or Shao Yao, to give her Chinese name when she was working as the deputy librarian in the Chinese provincial town of Fujinhaizhou[3].

Together, they had one child, Sean, now 18 years old. Tall and athletic, the boy had the black hair and good looks of a Eurasian to the point where some had referred to him as pretty. But Sean was not effeminate in any way. He excelled in sports, winning trophies and medals in rowing, fencing, and athletics. Besides, he had brought home adoring female friends several times, for which he appeared to have an endless supply.

---

[3] In *The Dragon's Threat*

Sean possessed a brilliant academic mind, focussing on developing Artificial Intelligence, and together with a couple of friends recently won a prestigious prize for a program that would present a three-dimensional hologram from a two-dimensional picture. Holroyd understood this was a major achievement because the program included a feature that adapted the result to reflect lifelike images.

Sean's achievement was recognised as impressive, and despite his youth, universities worldwide, including Cambridge, M.I.T., and Stanford, had offered him scholarships. He hadn't accepted any yet but was now hiking with friends through the Swiss Alps.

Thankfully, Holroyd had noted Sean was modest and seemed unaware or perhaps unconcerned with this recognition of his accomplishments.

Holroyd was impressed by his son but was unsure about his two colleagues. Rajeesh had come to England on a scholarship to study computer sciences and was considered a genius by many in his field. Black hair, slim, dark-skinned, with piercing black eyes and a smile that never seemed to disappear, Holroyd felt uneasy in his presence. He wondered if Rajeesh was hiding a ruthless personal ambition behind his smile. Viktor, on the other hand, was a different sort altogether.

As far as Holroyd knew, Viktor had arrived in England as a refugee from the Balkan wars and had decided to study applied computer sciences and had already built some interesting computer hardware for which he was awaiting patent approvals.

Tall, slim almost to the point of emaciation, with a sallow complexion and haunted look in his eyes that probably reflected his experiences in his native country, Viktor gave the impression of holding a brooding desire for revenge. The only question was on whom he hoped to exercise vengeance. However, he appeared to get on well with the other two, and Sean seemed comfortable working with both of them. *I may not be entirely comfortable, but these are the sort of people England needs these days.*

He returned to his thoughts of going to Mexico. *How am I going to persuade her? And I know no one there so how will I arrange my trip?*

Chapter 2

"Yes?" Meredith, 9th Viscount Hantington[4] or Merry to his friends, looked up from his desk as his secretary came in.

"The Cabinet Office just called, Sir," she reported. "The Cabinet Secretary would like a word with you."

"Any idea what it's about?" Merry asked.

"No, Sir."

"Inform them I'll be right over." Merry got up, glanced out the window, and walked swiftly to the Cabinet Office.

"Ah, Meredith," Sir John, the Cabinet Secretary, greeted him. "So good of you to drop by. Take a seat, will you?"

Merry sat as Sir John came straight to the point.

"I had a call from the Prime Minister." He waited for a response. When Merry said nothing, Sir John went on.

---

[4] An old school chum and now a senior British Civil servant for whom Holroyd has done work. (The Dragon's Threat and Gold Among the Trees)

"He's very concerned about the increased movement of illicit drugs into Britain. It's causing a strain on the police, the health, and social services, not to mention the number of deaths. Luckily, the media haven't picked up on the severity of the problem and we want to be sure they don't. At least not before we have a viable solution in place.

"Most of the drugs come from Mexico, and the National Crime Agency is requesting additional resources to expand their information network there and to increase their surveillance capacities here." He paused. "The Prime Minister is not convinced giving more resources will do much to improve the situation."

"Does he have any suggestions?"

"It's our responsibility to offer appropriate suggestions." Sir John looked balefully at Merry. "After all, that is what we are employed to do."

Merry was about to laugh out loud, but one look at Sir John convinced him that this was not the best time to be cavalier. Instead, he assumed a grave expression and nodded before asking, "And what does that have to do with me?"

"I'd like you to take over." Before Merry could reply, Sir John said, "I'm thinking you could take command, a sort of Drugs control Czar. You would coordinate information between departments with the authority to take or order action when you deem it necessary. But the main thing is to stop or at least reduce the flow of drugs." He looked sternly at Merry before continuing. "The Prime Minister wasn't particularly enthusiastic about the suggestion, but I assured him I have every confidence in you." He stopped. "I trust that confidence is not misplaced."

"Oh, it isn't," Merry started to reply.

"Oh, good. Just make sure it isn't." And with that, the meeting ended.

As Merry returned to his office, he wondered *how I am I supposed to do that?*

Chapter 3

Holroyd continued to sort through his files when he heard the phone ring and Pearl answered it to start a lengthy conversation in Chinese. *Family matters! Might be wise to steer clear in case it's bad news.* The call ended and Pearl came into the study.

"That was Wen Mei Li[5] She has been pro-moted to director in a different department." Pearl was happy at the news." We are very fortunate to have such a high official in our family." She stopped Then she announced. "I have to go home. Quan Li[6] is getting married, and there will be a big family gath-ering."

Holroyd's heart sank at the prospect of attend-ing the event, but he put on a smile.

"When are we going?" he asked.

"We?" Pearl looked puzzled. "*Bie choufengle!*" She switched to English. "Don't be crazy! You don't like such big social events, and everyone there will be speaking Chinese."

"But you said it's a family affair," Holroyd ob-served mildly.

---

[5] A distant relative who works for the Chinese State Security Bureau (Gold among the Trees)

[6] A distant nephew (Gold among the Trees)

"Oh, you only know my mother and Wen Mei Li So, you don't have to come with me. Perhaps when Sean is back, we can all go over, and he can meet his Chinese relatives. For now, don't worry! You can stay at home."

"With both you and Sean gone, I will be left alone. Perhaps I could go sightseeing while you are gone." Holroyd felt a surge of excitement at the prospect of getting Pearl's approval.

Pearl looked at him. "Just sightseeing?" she asked suspiciously.

"Yes, dear. Why else?"

"Where will you go?" Pearl's suspicion was clear by the tone of her voice.

"I haven't decided yet, but I thought I might go and look at the ancient buildings in Mexico," he replied artlessly.

Pearl didn't answer immediately but said, "Yes, that is a good idea." Then she said warningly. "But no more explorations that could get you into danger. Mexico is not a safe place, and you aren't as young as you once were."

"As always, you are right, *qinaide*" Holroyd admitted. "I promise I won't go anywhere dangerous or do anything that might get me into trouble."

"That's what you said when you went to China and again when you went to Canada. Each time you didn't keep that promise," Pearl retorted.

"I promise I will this time, dear."

Pearl considered his reply before relenting and asking, "Where will you stay? With whom will you meet?"

"I hadn't got that far, but I think Merry might be able to arrange some introductions."

"Ah yes! I have every faith in His Lordship," she said sarcastically, "*Nage ren bu kekao,*" before switching back to English, "he is not trustworthy."

"Darling! That's not fair."

"Yes, it is." She left the room.

Holroyd sat thinking over the exchange when the phone rang.

"Peter! *Ni hao!* I trust you are well." Wen Mei Li was calling.

"Wen Mei Li, I am well, thank you. I trust you are well too. Congratulations on your promotion; I am happy for you."

"Thank you, Peter, that is kind of you," Wen Mei Li answered.

"But let me get Pearl for you."

"Oh no! I am calling you," Wen interjected.

"Oh!" Holroyd was surprised.

"Pearl tells me you are planning a trip to Mexico. May I ask what the purpose of that trip is?"

Holroyd explained about wanting to go look at ancient ruins.

"And that is all?" Holroyd could hear her disbelief.

"I might do some sunbathing while I'm there."

"No other reason?"

"No. May I ask what this is about?"

"I am glad to hear that." Wen ignored his question. "I just want to warn you not to start living in interesting times again. *Zaijian*." The line went dead.

When the Chinese refer to interesting times, it usually means disasters or at least unpleasant experiences. So, what is Wen Mei Li telling me? Should I ask Pearl? But then it occurred to him that Pearl had passed on to Wen her fears about his trip, and he was being warned not to cause any worries. *Better let it lie.*

Holroyd postponed further research on Chinese voyages until after Pearl's departure and decided to call Merry.

Merry and Holroyd had gone to school together. If memory served, Merry had studied classics and left with a state scholarship, but their paths diverged after that. Holroyd joined the Navy, after which he went for academics.

The only thing Holroyd knew about what Merry had done after school was a vague notion he had gone into the Foreign Office. But he couldn't remember and didn't care about Merry's job. His photograph appeared occasionally in the social news, often in the company of a coterie of young women but never a wife.

"Hello, old boy," Merry answered, "I haven't heard from you for some time. What caused you to call?"

"I'm planning to go to Mexico," Holroyd explained, "specifically Acapulco. I don't know anyone down there and wondered if you had any contacts who might be helpful."

Merry paused before saying, "Come and join me for supper at the Athenaeum."

"Hang on, Merry! Every time we have supper there, you give me a task that I end up accepting only to end up in a mess," Holroyd protested. "This time, all I'm asking for is a name I can call upon."

"Oh, come on, old boy! "Merry protested. "I promise I have no hidden task for you."

"On that understanding, I'll gladly join you."

Chapter 4

Holroyd and Merry settled into their chairs in the dining room and ordered dinner, engaging in small talk as the meal was served.

"I saw your father has been promoted to a Dukedom. What does that mean for you?"

"Nothing at all, old boy." Merry laughed. "I don't think he's very pleased, but mother will be tickled pink. I remain just an ordinary viscount."

"But you'll inherit both titles, won't you?"

"I suppose so," Merry replied, "I haven't given it any thought."

"If you do, what do I have to call you?" Holroyd asked. "Your Eminence? Your Grace?"

"I'll let you know when we come to that bridge."

Dinner over, they went to the bar and ordered coffee and liqueurs. While waiting, they looked at each and Holroyd took the initiative by saying, "I don't know why you invited me to dine, but before you go too far, I won't accept anything like the last two jobs[7] you assigned me. I'm too old and besides, I'm totally committed to my family as well as planning for my retirement."

---

[7] The Dragon's Threat and Gold Among the Trees

"I see," Merry replied. "And what will you be do-ing?"

"As I told you. I'm planning to go to Mexico, Acapulco, to be precise. I want to see if the stele I was told about is Chinese." He took a sip of wine. "I have no contacts there and so no idea where to stay or whom to contact."

"Surely, your travel agent will help you there."

"Merry! I don't use travel agents. What they arrange is never satisfactory, and the last thing I want to do is to mingle with tourists, pay exorbitant prices, and start knocking on doors to get information."

Holroyd noticed a slight smile on Merry's face and uncomfortably shifted in his chair.

"I quite sympathise with you," Merry observed soothingly, although Holroyd suspected sympathy was not in Merry's dictionary.

There was silence as Holroyd realised Merry was enjoying Holroyd's disquiet and was waiting for Holroyd to ask for help. Resignedly accepting that Merry now held the upper hand, Holroyd meekly asked, "Can you help me?"

"I think I might be able to," Merry replied, savouring his victory. He raised his glass, examining the rich colour of the content before continuing. "We don't have a consul there since the last one came down with dengue fever or some such. But I think I can have a word with the Spanish Embassy here, and they could pass the word to their man in Acapulco." He stopped. "You did a great favour for one of their noble families as I recall. What were they called?"

"The de Perrefaltas," Holroyd offered.

"Right! You might be able to call in that favour if you need to," Merry noted and continued, "as it happens, there is an old school chum of ours living there. You might remember him, his name was Smythe-Jones Minor."

Holroyd shook his head.

"Doesn't matter," Merry observed. "Anyway, he took the cloth and has been doing parishioner work in the slums down there for decades. He might be of use to you." He looked at Holroyd, before saying enticingly. "I could give him a call."

Holroyd sensed there might be at least one condition lurking behind that suggestion. *Alright, let's see what Merry wants this time.* He took a swallow from his glass and looked directly at Merry.

"What aren't you telling me?"

Merry didn't answer the question but instead said, "What do you know about the Mexican drug trade?"

"Nothing," Holroyd replied. "That's way out of my field of interest."

"I know that old boy," Merry acknowledged, "but let me tell you a bit about it."

"Come off it, Merry," Holroyd protested, "I told you I have no interest in that."

"Give me a chance, old boy," Merry admonished. "Let me give you an overview before you react."

"Oh, very well," Holroyd said resignedly.

"Illicit drugs such as methamphetamine, heroin, and cocaine coming into Britain often arrive here from Mexico. Some of it comes directly, but much comes via other countries, including Europe and the United States." He stopped to take a swallow. "It's an enormous problem, but one way to help deal with it would be to stop exportation from Mexico."

"We know that a lot of the drugs come from Asia and are first shipped to Mexican ports including Acapulco. Acapulco is both the sixth deadliest city in Mexico and the seventh-deadliest city in the world; the US government has warned its citizens not to travel there. In September 2018, the city's entire police force was disarmed by the military due to suspicions that drug gangs had infiltrated it." Merry took another swallow from his glass.

"That's all very interesting but what's this about, Merry?" Holroyd replied. "And why are you telling me this? And what do you expect me to do?"

"I need your help regarding the inflow of illegal drugs into Britain," Merry said.

"The movement of drugs into Britain?" Holroyd was surprised. "How on earth do you think I know anything about that? How could I possibly help you?"

"Oh! Not directly, of course," Merry tried to re-assure Holroyd. "But not all problems can be solved by direct action."

"I conclude from that, that you want me to do something that's indirect." Holroyd said, "And what does this indirect action require me to do?"

"Establish for me a means of communication with someone you know," Merry said.

"Why would I be able to do that?" asked Holroyd.

Merry answered. "You met with one of the people we have our eye on." He stopped again before looking at Holroyd and saying, " Li Feng."

"You want me to set up a channel of communication for you, with Li Feng?" Holroyd was taken by surprise. "I have met him, but that had nothing to do with drugs. That was all about finding Koxinga's treasure."

"Yes. But you met him," Merry pointed out.

"How does that have anything to do with the movement of drugs?"

"Probably nothing. But in this game, even a casual meeting is suspicious."

"Hang on, Merry," Holroyd protested. "Am I hearing you right? Are you implying I'm involved in the drug trade?"

"I'm not," Merry replied. "I know you too well. But others are involved, not all of whom know you as well as I do."

"Who?"

"Western drug enforcement people and your contacts in the Chinese State Security Bureau."

"What? Wen Mei Li or Li Wen Yao?" Holroyd sat up worried. "Are they after me again? Is this what it's all about?" *Is that why Wen Mei Li called me?*

"Oh, no. Don't get so hot under the collar," Merry laughed.

"Then what?"

"I wondered if you could arrange some introductions."

"Anyone in particular?" asked Holroyd.

"Yes, the woman Wen Mei Li," Merry said, " I believe she's a distant relative of yours."

Holroyd sat back, taken aback. "I'm not sure how she will respond. But why me? Surely there are official channels that would be more effective," Holroyd said.

"Not sure if we can trust them. There are signs they might be leaking, but we don't know where," Merry explained.

"So, are you looking to plug the leak or bypass it until you can find it?" Holroyd asked.

"We'd prefer to plug it, of course. But that will take time we don't think we have. So, to be safe, we want an under-the-radar bypass."

"And you think Wen Mei Li would agree to work that way," Holroyd said.

"Yes."

Holroyd considered what he had heard. *This isn't like Merry. There has to be more than just setting up a contact.* Finally, with a sinking heart, he asked, "Anything else?"

"Well, if you're going down there," Merry grinned, "I'd like you to meet and have a chat with someone who's of interest to us. I think then we would be able to cover some of your expenses."

"Just meet and have a chat and no more," Holroyd echoed. "Would we have an agreement?"

"Definitely, old boy."

***

Once home, Holroyd let Pearl know of Merry's request, but her response was lukewarm.

"Wen Mei Li will say this is not following normal procedure and could reflect badly on her. Before she would do anything, she would want to know what benefit there is for her and the family," she said.

"Ask her to allow Merry to call her," Holroyd suggested. "Let them discuss the matter unofficially."

But Pearl seemed unconvinced. Holroyd let the matter drop, guessing that once in China, Pearl would raise the matter privately. If she didn't, there was nothing he could do.

Pearl went out of the room but returned shortly to announce her departure and to report she had been in contact with Wen Mei Li.

"She is not pleased."

Holroyd understood that he would be held responsible for any problems the contact might cause. *I wonder if I did the right thing. But it's too late now.*

Chapter 5

Mickie had trouble in starting the car, an old Ford, which made her even more irritable as she drove to her office. She drove carefully, mindful of the early morning rush hour traffic, and mulled over the program for the day. Monday morning was always fraught with possibilities because one never really knew what the weekend might have produced.

She parked her car and entered the old office building, a relic of Canada's days as a Dominion. High ceilings, stone floors, dark and polished wood panelling, and glass doors proclaimed the majesty of Imperial officialdom at the expense of efficiency. In case no one noticed this characteristic, ubiquitous portraits and marble busts of long-gone officers provided a reminder.

In those days, stuffy British Colonial officials jostled in the corridors with lumber barons, sea captains, and newly arrived settlers, but those days had gone. Developers had taken ownership of the building about ten years ago, but they had yet to see fit to modernize it. Sometimes, Mickie wondered whether that was a sign of the owner's parsimony or respect for history.

Mickie climbed to her second-floor cubicle and then went over to the Editor's office.

Editor John Breckenridge's persona had earned him the nickname of the Count. His generous and well-tended silvery hair gave him an aura of graciousness that accentuated the finely drawn lines of his face. Grey-green eyes would watch warily without his glasses to hide them, while a ready smile could conceal an ability to act ruthlessly.

A man of action, often hot-tempered, though generally sympathetic, and sensitive, the Count commanded total respect for his five feet four inches of pure driving energy, whether liked or hated.

"Morning, Mickie. Hope you had a good weekend," Breckenridge welcomed her. Mickie nodded. "Shut the door, will you? Sit down. The owner called me and wants us to do an immediate in-depth piece on the movement of illicit drugs. He wants the whole picture, the why's, the how's, and the outcomes." He stopped. "I know you feel passionately about the problems in society today, but there hasn't been an opportunity to assign you something in that field. But I think this is something you'll find challenging.

He watched her reaction. Seeing a gleam in her eyes, he continued, "The owner is mostly interested in how our government reacts, but I leave it to you how you handle it. Anyway, he wants to know who will be assigned, and if you're interested, I'll put your name forward."

"As I said, I know nothing of that." Mickie paused before continuing. "But it sounds intriguing."

"I have every confidence you'll do well," Breckenridge remarked encouragingly.

"Then, yes, put my name forward.," she said excitedly. *I've been waiting for something like this. It's my chance to get known!*

"Good. Just let me get the background." He rummaged in a desk drawer, picked up a folder file, glanced at it briefly, and pushed it over to her.

Shortly afterwards, she was told she had the assignment.

Back at her desk, Mickie looked over the folders on her desk, each representing a case file of some local interest story. She pushed them aside and began surfing the net to see what she could find about the illegal drug trade.

Chapter 6

"Peter, how are you?" Wen Mei Li's voice floated down the line.

"Wen Mei Li! I am fine, thank you. I hope all is well with you also. How may I help you?"

"Pearl has arrived safely and told me of your request," Wen answered. "I am curious that your friend wants to establish what I would only class as unofficial contacts with us. I find that very strange and want to know why."

"Yes, I found it strange also," Holroyd admitted. Then he said, "He didn't tell me the full story, but it has to do with the movement of illegal drugs from Asia and Mexico to Britain."

"The movement of drugs?" There was silence before Wen Mei Li continued, "Peter, I warned you about living in interesting times. Please follow my advice."

"Wen Mei Li, I will most certainly do so," Holroyd answered sincerely. "Meanwhile, what may I tell my friend?"

"You may tell him to get in touch with me," Wen Mei Li answered, "Again, Peter, be careful. People in the drug trade are dangerous, and if you become a person of interest to them, we may not be able to help you. You have a family to care for. That should be the focus of your activities. *Zai dian.* " And the line went dead.

"Bye," Holroyd answered. Danger? *Either Merry hasn't fully briefed me, which would be normal for him, or Wen Mei Li is reflecting Pearl's concerns. There's no danger. After all, I'm only going to look for a stele. I don't think meeting with Merry's people would get me involved in the drug trade.*

Holroyd began to plan his trip when Merry called to say that he had talked with Smythe-Jones Minor.

"Doesn't remember you," he reported, "But he'll gladly put you up. Just don't expect five-star accommodation. Remember, he is a missionary down there now. Those people tend to live modestly."

After Holroyd thanked him, Merry continued, "Oh, I also mentioned your trip to the Spanish ambassador here, and he will pass it on to Acapulco. You'll probably be invited to meet their local representative." With that, the call ended.

Holroyd emailed Sean advising him of the arrangements. However, Sean did not send an acknowledgement, but Holroyd was not worried, thinking Sean was too busy or already underway.

Chapter 7

Mickie decided to start from the beginning and learned that Mexico is the world's richest country in hallucinogenic drugs.

Mexico became a major player in the international trafficking of narcotics in the early 20th Century but at the time was considered to be largely irrelevant to the global narcotics trade.

That changed when the United States Congress passed the Opium Exclusion Act, a law that prohibited the importation of opium into the United States. That legislation, combined with opium-market upheavals in Asia caused by the 1907 Sino-British Agreement, almost instantly turned Mexico into a major supplier of illicit opium to its neighbour north of the border.

World War II, which cut off traditional supplies of opiates to the Western Hemisphere, provided new opportunities for Mexican opium growers to fill the gap.

That production came increasingly under the control of growers and traffickers in northwest Mexico who were in cahoots with politicians, police, and military officials.

After the end of the war, leadership in drug control was transferred from the public health authorities to the attorney general's office. At the same time, the army and other Mexican security forces, especially the (eventually notorious) Directorate of Federal Security (DFS), were given greater roles in the fight against illicit narcotics.

The creation of the DFS enabled the Mexican state to control drug trafficking more systematically. This system had two objectives: it ensured that influential state actors could skim profits from the increasingly lucrative trade, and it helped keep the traffickers under control and out of politics.

At the start of the 21st Century, a declaration of 'war' on the traffickers, spiralled Mexico into an orgy of violence and atrocities, complete with decapitations, mass graves, and increasing evidence that the state simply is no longer able to control the *narcos.*

Despite the 'war,' drugs continue to flow into the United States and other countries, while arms are smuggled back south to carry out the killings, to the tune of perhaps 200,000 dead over the next 15 years. *Clearly, then, that war doesn't do much to stop the movement of drugs.*

The American government has a major interest in stopping the Mexican drug trade but is limited in finding an acceptable solution. Whereas there is support for military action and declaring war on the cartels, the idea that the problem would be solved is delusional.

The Mexican government has adamantly refused to use the US military in solving the country's drug problem. Thus, incursion of American forces without Mexican government approval would be an act of war.

Even if the Mexicans agreed to invite American forces, the outcome is unlikely to stop the drug trade. If the Americans, after 20 years, couldn't stop the trade in Afghanistan, what chance of success would they have in Mexico, where the cartels operate in large areas of no man's land, are massively funded, possess armed militias, and have access to modern transportation?

Mickie sat back considering whether to go to Mexico to see for herself. *What's good journalism if it's all based on other people's reports that probably include personal biases when interpreting facts?*

She was conscious of the warnings about tourism and went to the media and social networks to see if there was anything useful to know. As she spooled over the pages, she saw an article in a Mexican newspaper. Her Spanish was good enough to understand the article's essence but not all the details.

It was about a group of British hikers who had to be rescued off a Swiss glacier when the weather turned bad. She noted the word *muertos* but could not follow to whom it referred. *Probably in this paper as a filler.*

Just as she was about to turn to the next page, she caught the name Sean Holroyd among the names, and that name rang a bell. *Holroyd? Holroyd is an unusual name. Still, I don't think it has any relevance to the drugs trade.* She continued to spool, but the name kept distracting her, like a buzzing insect in the bedroom at night.

The distraction continued, and she stopped her research and went to her own newspaper's archives to discover that Professor Peter Holroyd had been involved in the hunt for Koxinga's gold and the murder of both an indigenous woman and a prominent local philanthropist[8]. *Professor Holroyd has quite a background. Given he's been implicated in gold and murder, I wonder if he's also involved in the drug trade. If he is, it would give a local, perhaps even sensational, twist to the story. It's a long shot, but who knows what I might find.*

She considered her logic. *There's nothing to suggest he's involved with drugs but given his past it's conceivable.* Thinking how to proceed, she realised the report of the Holroyd involved in the Swiss accident might be an approach. *I think a call is in order.*

---

[8] Gold among the Trees

Chapter 8

"Professor Holroyd?" she asked when Holroyd answered the call. "My name is Jeanne-Michelle Desforestier, and I am a journalist in Victoria, Canada."

"Yes?"

"Before I continue, may I just make sure I'm speaking to the correct person," Mickie went on. "Are you the Professor Holroyd who was at the university here some years ago?"

"I am," Holroyd confirmed. "May I ask, Miss Desforestier, what this is about?" *Why did she raise my stay at the university? Is she going muckraking by opening all that again?*

"Oh, please call me Mickie," she laughed. "I came across a newspaper report and noticed a reference to Sean Holroyd. Is he a relative?"

"My son is called Sean. He's hiking with some friends in the Alps right now." Holroyd paused. *What is she about? Does she know something I should know?*

There was a pause as Mickie realised that Holroyd was unaware of the incident in Switzerland. *Oh my God, he doesn't know his son is dead. Well, I'm not going to tell him.*

"So, you're not worried," Mickie insisted.

"Mickie, any expedition, or Alpine hike can expect to meet dangers. Of course, I'm worried as I would be for any expedition, but if the idea is to avoid any danger, then no expedition would ever go."

"Are you planning to go over there?"

"No, why should I?" Holroyd asked but Mickie said nothing. Holroyd went on, "I have other plans in mind. My wife is away and rather than sit at home alone, I think I could use a holiday in the sun on a beach."

"Do you have any particular beach in mind?" Mickie asked.

"Not yet," replied Holroyd, "but I hear Acapulco is reportedly offering such a beach." *What's this about? Surely, she's not suggesting she wants to come along. Pearl would have my head served on a platter if I even thought of pursuing the idea. No! You, young lady, are not coming with me.*

"And is that the only reason for you to choose Acapulco?"

"No," Holroyd laughed. "There's a report of a monument near there that's of interest to me."

"May I ask what monument?"

"It's a report of a column that looks like it might be a Chinese stele," Holroyd answered and explained his interest.

"I see," Mickie remarked. "I wish you luck in your search. Who knows, perhaps we will run across each other one day." And with that, the call ended.

Holroyd replaced the phone, sat back, and reviewed the phone call. *What was that about? Why would she call me? Does she know something that I should know? And why should I be worried about Sean? I'll give him a call to make sure.* There was no answer. *Probably no signal where he is. I'll try again later*

Mickie thought over the call. *He hasn't heard about his son. He's going to be devastated when he finds out what happened. He's going to Mexico to look for some artifact, but I don't think he's telling me everything. So, what could he be hiding? I think I may have struck gold; I think he is involved in drugs. I'm going to look closer at Professor Peter Holroyd.*

She returned to the archives of her own paper and searched for references to Holroyd. The archives needed to be completed, but she found several interesting articles.

One reported Holroyd's outburst when a colleague, Paul van Vervoort, reported finding an ancient skeleton and some valuable artifacts. In a few words, van Vervoort had dismissed Holroyd as a fake. In another article, van Vervoort laid the blame squarely on Holroyd for a standoff on the nearby reservation.

Another article claimed the university had raised doubts about Holroyd's academic achievements. A final article reported Holroyd had been arrested on suspicion of the murder of a local philanthropist.

Well, well! Look what you find if you dig deep enough. Professor Holroyd going to Mexico with a background like that makes me wonder, why you're really going down there. You have now become a person of interest to me. She shivered with a surge of anticipation akin to a predator sighting prey.

"I wonder if anyone is still around," she mused and started phoning her contacts. She drew a blank at first, but then she was informed that Inspector Watson, formerly with the Victoria police, had been the officer handling the case of the murder of the philanthropist. He was now retired living in a retirement home. A request to interview the Inspector was granted and Mickie went out there.

On arrival and once introductions had been made and Mickie explained why she wanted the interview.

"What do you remember about the Professor, Peter Holroyd?" she asked.

"Oh, him," Watson answered. "We had him in our sights as prime suspect for the murder., but in the end he was cleared," and he explained the circumstances. "But there were some loose ends that we never did solve."

"Can you explain that?"

"Part of the mystery was the nature of his connections with a couple of Chinese guys. He claimed that there was none, but as I remember, that was not what the Chinese police told us."

Mickie sat up and leaned forward with expectation. *So, Professor, there is more to you than what's in the public domain.* "Why was further questioning necessary?"

"We were asked to extradite the Chinamen to be tried in China for dealing drugs to the Americas. We never investigated that aspect of their activities. But when the extradition papers arrived, it was too late," answered Watson.

"How so? Asked Mickie.

Watson thought for a moment before answering. "We couldn't follow up because one of the two was assassinated, and the other left the country before we could question him again."

"But Holroyd was involved with them?" she insisted. "Are you sure of that?"

"Oh yes. Both Holroyd and the Chinamen admitted as much," he said.

Mickie sat up straight and almost shouted with satisfaction but controlled herself and smiled instead. *Eureka! This is huge! I may have got a scoop!*

Watson interrupted her joy, "But there was something else."

"What?" Suddenly wary that her pleasure may have been premature, Mickie slouched back in her chair, all sense of satisfaction evaporating faster than snow in the Sahara..

"There was a Chinese Police Officer here," he said and stopped. Then he went on. "She vouched for him, and I never could understand why. As far as I was told, he wasn't exactly popular over there, so why would she have stood up for him?"

"Did you come to some conclusion?"

"No," Watson replied, "But then I wondered if there wasn't more to her. Could they be collaborators? She told us she was involved in catching drug dealers, and I asked myself if Holroyd was also involved in drugs." *Eureka!* But Mickie hid her elation.

Mickie thanked Watson and returned to her office. Once there, she resumed her search and discovered Holroyd had once taken a leave of absence from his English university after publishing a paper roundly criticized as specious. While on leave, he had been arrested and deported from China on the grounds he had engaged in the tomb-robbing trade.

"After all that, you manage to be given tenure at your university. How is that possible unless you have some very powerful friends?" she muttered. "And now you are visiting Mexico to look at a supposed ancient Chinese monument! I don't think so! Professor, you, and your powerful friends aren't as clean as you would have us believe." She reached for the phone and called the Count.

"John, I think I might have a good story." She said, "I think we have a local story that goes back a few years and was never resolved. I think there were some cover-ups by people in very high places, and those people may be involved in the drug trade." She detailed the results of her research on Holroyd. "I'd like to run with this."

"Mickie, you have your assignment." Breckenridge replied, "Don't get distracted and lose sight of that."

"I think Holroyd is somehow involved in the drug trade," she countered, "and I think the involvement reaches into China and England. I smell corruption in high places. And the links may lead back to Holroyd. I don't think he's what he pretends to be." There was silence.

"Is that so?" Breckenridge said. "Ok. Let me check with the owner, and I'll get back to you." A few minutes later, the phone rang.

"The owner likes it, so go ahead and run with it but make sure you've got your facts right   and they're verifiable before putting anything down. I don't have to tell you the consequences of being wrong."

"Don't worry, I'll make sure," Mickie replied, "But this is going to be huge."

***

In Vancouver, Simon O'Mallory, owner of the paper, put the phone down and smiled. He remembered Holroyd all too well. Holroyd was suspected as the murderer of his father and had tried to extort money by threatening to reveal where Koxinga's gold was hidden. *Revenge is sweet!*

Chapter 9

Holroyd exited from Acapulco's arrival area and looked for someone among the welcoming crowd holding his name on a placard. He did not see one and, given Merry had not passed on an address or a telephone number for Smythe-Jones,

Holroyd debated what to do next. He stepped out of the air-conditioned Airport terminal into the tropical heat that a desultory offshore breeze hardly dented, looking for a taxi. He already felt sweaty and regretted not having dressed for his arrival. He wiped his face with a handkerchief and waved at a taxi that obligingly moved up to him and opened the door to get in.

"Holroyd?" A man dressed in shorts and a T-shirt came up to him. "I say, I'm terribly sorry not to have arrived sooner, but I'm here now. Let me take your bag, and I see you flagged a taxi. Well done."

"Thanks for coming. I was beginning to feel lost," Holroyd had no time to answer more before they were in the taxi and off to whatever accommodation Smythe-Jones had arranged.

"Merry told me about your quest," Smythe-Jones remarked. "He also told me you'd be like a lost child down here and asked for my help." Holroyd gave an assenting nod.

"I'm not sure exactly what you need or how I can help," Smythe-Jones said, "but we can discuss that later. Meanwhile, you're welcome to stay with me. It's not five stars, but it's airconditioned, the plumbing's reasonable, I have internet, and the electricity usually works. But if you'd prefer, I can book you into one of the hotels here."

"No, No! I'd be delighted to stay with you."

"Great!" Smythe-Jones answered. "Once we get there, get yourself settled, and when you're ready, we can go round the corner to a small cantina I usually go to. The staff and the food are great, but don't drink the water."

Showered and changed, Holroyd went down to go to the cantina.

"Washed, rested, and ready to go, Vicar," he announced.

"Oh! I'm not a vicar or a father, come to that." Smythe-Jones laughed. "Here, I'm known as Brother Philip. Call me Philip, but I draw the line if you call me Pip."

"Then Philip it is, and please call me Peter."

"Oh, by the way," Philip said, "This arrived for you while you were upstairs." And he handed over a letter.

"That's odd, I didn't think anyone knew I was going to be coming or staying here." Holroyd took the letter and saw that it was heavily embossed with the Spanish Coat of Arms under which *Cónsul general española en Acapulco* was written. Inside was an invitation to an evening reception at the Consulate the next day. A handwritten addendum signed by Don Luis de Perrefalta welcomed him to Acapulco. No RSVP was required.

"Oh! How nice," Holroyd explained his connection with the de Perrefaltas. "Do you want to come along? I doubt anyone would mind."

"Better not," Philip answered, "They are rather sticky about protocol and if they wanted me to come, they would have said so."

Together they went to the cantina where Maria welcomed them with a "Brother Philip. Welcome to you and your guest." She smiled and continued, "An old friend from *Inglaterra*?" She came over to the table. "*Si*! He is too pale to be from anywhere else." She patted Holroyd on the shoulder and asked, "*Un cafecito* y *una galleta* as usual, Brother Philip?"

"Not this time, Maria," Philip laughed. "Two Coronas and nachos to start, please. And then we'll decide what else."

"Miguel will bring them over," Maria nodded and went to give the order.

"So, Merry gave me some idea what you're here for," Philip opened the conversation.

"That's not my main purpose. In coming here," Holroyd said and launched into his reasons for coming to Acapulco. "I am only interested in finding that stele the Vatican mentioned, and any help you can give me will be much appreciated." He paused as if deciding to say something but continued, "Anything else, including Merry's requests, are incidental, and I won't let them interfere with my search"

Philip listened attentively and said, "Let me do some research at the Archdiocese. Even though we are of different beliefs, we do get on very well and they appreciate what I try to do here to help the poor. After all, poverty and sickness are not the preserve of any one faith."

"That would be very helpful," Holroyd replied.

"So, for what was it that Merry wanted your help?"

"Oh, yes," Holroyd answered just as Miguel approached the table. Unaware that Miguel was close enough to hear, Holroyd continued, "Merry is looking at the traffic in drugs from China."

Miguel put the beers and the plate of nachos on the table and left.

"Damn!" Philip watched Miguel going to the back of the cantina. "I saw him twitch when you mentioned drugs. We never discuss the drug trade when in a public place because you never know who is listening and to whom they then report."

"Isn't Miguel trusted?"

"He started here a couple of months ago," answered Philip, still looking toward the back of the room. "I don't know anything about him, and that means I don't trust him."

Maria came over, "Have you decided on dinner?"

Chapter 10

The Spanish Honorary Consul's residence was in the colonial era Spanish Governor's Palace. On entering, Holroyd had the feeling not much had changed. The architecture and furnishings testified to the opulent tastes of Spanish Grandees of that bygone era, and the liveried footmen in powdered wigs perpetuated the illusion.

Holroyd never liked going to formal social functions and felt uncomfortable as he was led through the ballroom to the patio where a magnificent buffet was laid out. The footman stopped at the entrance to the patio and announced his name in a stentorian bellow. Holroyd looked at the footman in surprise and stopped not knowing if he should walk on or wait for someone to come and greet him. As he stood there looking around the patio wondering what to do next, a small man came over with an outstretched hand.

"Doctor Holroyd," he greeted, "I am so glad you could come. I am Don Luis de Perrefalta, Spanish Consul General here. It is my honour to meet you, sir."

"The honour is entirely mine, sir," Holroyd replied, "thank you for inviting me."

"After your service to my family, Professor, I could do no less," Don Luis said sincerely and went on, "Besides, I received a request from Madrid to be ready to help you should you need it. As such, it is also a duty and one that I will gladly fulfill." He took Holroyd by the arm. "Come, let me introduce you to the other guests."

After a series of meaningless introductions, Holroyd was introduced to an American who could have been a football linebacker.

"Professor Holroyd," the man said, "I'm Charles Strang. It's an honour to meet you in person finally."

"I'm sorry," Holroyd was surprised. "Have we communicated in some way?"

"Oh, no!" Strang replied. "But I am aware of your exploits in China."

Before Holroyd could answer, he heard, "Professor Holroyd! How nice to meet you." Holroyd turned to see a young black lady coming towards him.

"I'm Mickie," she said.

"I didn't expect to meet you here," Holroyd was taken aback.

"Miss Desforestier has been telling me all about your interests here in Mexico," Strang interjected. "I think, Professor, you and I might have similar interests."

"Really?" Holroyd was puzzled. "You have an interest in ancient Chinese monuments?"

"Not at all," Strang answered. "I was referring to transpacific trade matters. Why not stop by my office, and let's exchange information."

Who is this man? Why would he want to talk with me about something I do not know or do not intend to discuss?

"But unless ancient Chinese trade is involved, I have no interest in transpacific trade matters," Holroyd protested. He noted how Strang and Mickie exchanged quick looks. *Have those two been talking about me? If so, what did who tell whom?*

"Somehow, I just don't quite believe you." And Strang went to mingle with other guests.

"Who is he?" Holroyd wondered.

"He's the local American spook," Mickie answered, "He's with CIA or DEA or something."

"How would you know that?" Holroyd turned to her.

Mickie just grinned and disappeared into the crowd.

"Journalists! How come they always seem to know something no one else knows? Just lovely! "Holroyd muttered to himself. "And now some American mystery official doesn't approve of me. I've been there before, and I hated it." *What's going on here? What has Mickie been telling Strang, and why does he want to talk to me? I'm here to find that stele and talk to people Merry wants me to meet. None of that should have excited a journalist or some American official. More to the point, has Merry landed me in a mess again?*

As soon as he felt he could, he thanked his host and took his leave. Once back at Philip's home, he tried to reach Sean, but again, there was no answer. *That's strange. He usually replies quite quickly.*

***

"There are disturbing whispers in the court-yards," the caller said. "Our friends in Ho Chi Min City request corrective action."

"I was unaware of any such reports," the receiver answered, "May I know what troubles our friends?"

"Some old acquaintances of yours have become active again, which is irritating. Any moves to stop them would be seen as a sign of your continued co-operation."

"I am surprised my cooperation was in question." The receiver shifted nervously in his chair.

"Let us ensure it never will be," the caller observed. "Our little whisperers tell us that Wen Mei Li has been in contact with your old nemesis Holroyd and through him with the British nobleman. We want to know if they are looking in corners we prefer they should not."

"Yes, I fully understand. I may have some corrective actions I can initiate."

"That would be most appreciated." And the line went dead.

The receiver sat back and then called Bangkok.

Chapter 11

Song Wharatsaphut pushed past his friend Siva and peeped out from behind the curtain by the side of the stage to cast a quick view over the club's main room. The bar was full this evening, mostly foreigners but a couple of Asians, all eager to see the show and for a few to get some private action. There was a hum of conversation and an air of expectancy as the patrons waited for the show to begin.

In daylight, the club would be seen as an empty place with tawdry decorations, smelling of stale beer, tobacco, and cheap colognes. But that changed at night when soft lighting hid the garishness of the settings, the sound of music, and the clink of glasses replaced the silence of the day, although the night's clientele did reinforce the smells. Then, the purpose of the establishment would become clear. Here, sex was on display and available for the right price.

Song was tall and big-boned for a Thai, and he was strikingly handsome in a way that attracted both men and women. But on closer inspection, his eyes had a deadness that smiles, and laughter could not hide.

No one meeting him for the first time would feel empathy but could sense a longing for genuine emotions of friendship and warmth. Some people might even sense somewhere inside him was a loveable human being, but few did because it was hidden behind a carapace born of hardship and betrayal.

However, such people would never visit an establishment like this one.

Song took another look at the room. In a far corner of the bar, Lieutenant Thanaphon of the Vice Squad was sitting at a table by himself with a half glass of beer. He was here for his usual payment, and Song watched the manager give an envelope to the Lieutenant. Thanaphon took the envelope, opened it, and, glancing inside, nodded at the manager.

Song stepped back and made room for four boys in skimpy bikinis pinned with flamboyant numbers who stood, strutted, and pirouetted across the brightly lit stage. Every five minutes or so the quartet would be replaced by another similarly dressed four. Sometimes, the clientele would glance at the stage before losing interest and resuming their conversations; at other times, a parade would be greeted with clapping and shouts of approval.

At one table, a solitary man called a waiter over and whispered something at which one of the actors was called off the stage and accompanied to the table to make the man's acquaintance. That was the usual routine, but sometimes it varied if the two left the barroom and went behind a curtain by the side of the stage, only to reappear half an hour or an hour later.

Another quartet, another invitation, and a disappearance behind the curtain. Thanaphon was satisfied all was routine, yawned and debated whether to order another beer. He noted a waiter came out from behind the curtain and looked frantically for the manager. The two men walked hurriedly behind the curtain, and for a few minutes, nothing happened. Thanaphon thought no more about it, stood up and was about to leave when the manager came over to him sweating and looking very disturbed.

"Lieutenant, please, you must come. There has been a terrible accident." The man was almost incoherent and clutching piteously at the lieutenant's arm.

"What?" Thanaphon responded irritably, annoyed at the delay. However, the manager tugged at his arm, and Thanaphon became aware that some clients began noticing. Grudgingly, he followed the manager behind the curtain into a narrow, dimly red-lit passage with curtained-off spaces on either side. They stopped at one such space, and Thanaphon looked inside.

The space was sparsely furnished with a narrow bed, a chair, and a small table on which could be seen lubricants, a candle stub, a half-empty bottle of whiskey, and a glass tumbler.

Huddled in one corner with a terrified look and tears running down his cheeks was the young man Thanaphon recognized as Song. On the bed lay a naked middle-aged white male. Thanaphon pushed past the manager and shook the man by the shoulder but reached for the man's pulse when there was no response.

"He's dead! What happened?" The manager looked at the boy. "Well?"

Still crying, Song detailed how the encounter had gone predictably until the man started convulsing. Song had called for help, but the man stopped moving before anyone arrived.

Thanaphon asked a couple of questions before reaching for the man's belongings. He found a wallet with no money or credit cards, some bills and ticket stubs, an electronic hotel room card, and an American driver's license.

"I don't see a watch, cell phone, or passport; his money is gone." The Lieutenant looked at Song and then at the manager meaningfully, who shuffled nervously but said nothing. Thanaphon waited.

"Well?" Thanaphon asked, "If they're not on him or in the room, someone must have taken them." The manager still said nothing. "I see." He looked menacingly at the manager. "This can go down one of two ways."

The manager nodded and resignedly invited Thanaphon into the office. Once there, he opened the safe and took out a wad of money that Thanaphon counted carefully. More money changed hands.

"Get your people to throw the body out into an alley that's not near here. Make sure there are no identifying marks, but an overdose injection would help to make the paperwork easier when the corpse is found. And clean up that cubicle before anyone else gets to use it."

"And the boy?"

Just then, Thanaphon's cell phone chimed. After a short conversation, Thanaphon shut his phone and looked at the shaken manager.

"Keep him up somewhere safe and make sure is well looked after and healthy," he ordered, "I may have use of him." And with that, Thanaphon left, leaving the manager puzzled and sitting forlornly in the office.

Meanwhile, Song was left alone in the dark. Exhausted by the experience and fear, he finally fell asleep, only to be woken by the manager at what was probably near dawn.

"Get up and come out of there." The manager beckoned Song out of the cupboard. "Put these clothes on and come with me." Song was taken downstairs and handed over to Lieutenant Thanaphon.

Thanaphon looked at Song and said, "You're going to England."

Chapter 12

Merry woke with a thundering headache and the mother of all hangovers. He had difficulty focusing his eyes; the room seemed to spin around him, there was a vile taste in his mouth, and his head harboured a loud pounding. He groaned and tried to remember the events of the previous evening.

He had gone over to his usual club, where he played cards. He had started well, but from then on had progressed from bad to worse. He'd lost his initial winnings and continued to lose, until the manager had come over to suggest he had better stop until his debts were cleared.

He had moved to the bar to mull over his options when the club manager appeared at his side again.

"May I introduce Mr. Cheng Fu, my lord?" Merry turned to see a Chinese man who asked, "May I join your lordship?"

"Why?"

"I have an offer to make to you," Cheng replied.

"It's one that's very generous, my lord," the manager intervened, "and one I suggest you consider seriously."

"I see," Merry looked at Cheng. "Well then, let me hear it."

Together, they had moved to an alcove where a waiter brought a drink for Merry and a glass of juice for Cheng. After some small talk, Cheng got to the point. In short, Cheng offered Merry a substantial amount of money, which his lordship doubtlessly could find useful if his Lordship could do a small favour in return.

"What is this small favour?" Merry asked, slurring his voice a little.

"We would like you to divert your energies in a different direction," Cheng said.

Slightly inebriated and not thinking straight, Merry looked at him, "I say, old boy, what are you talking about?"

"I understand you are involved in examining one aspect of transpacific trade," Cheng explained. "We suggest there are better-qualified people to undertake this task."

"And you want to give me money so that I will let these better-qualified people do my job?" Merry waited until Cheng nodded and said, "Sorry old boy, wrong address." And he moved back to the bar not noticing Cheng was placing a call on his cellphone.

***

The door opened, and Soames, his valet, entered, stopping Merry's efforts to reconstruct the night before.

"Good morning, my lord." Soames put a tray with the tea, newspaper, and a brown paper envelope on Merry's bed and drew the curtains back to reveal a gloriously sunny day.

Merry groaned and blinked, wondering whether the headache was worse than the one he had suffered yesterday, and his mouth tasted like…… what? He could sense his hand was trembling, and he wondered whether he should throw up, but decided it was too much effort.

"Water, aspirin, whatever." he croaked.

"Hair of the dog, m'lord?"

"Just do whatever you need to make me feel human, dammit."

"Indeed, m'lord."

"What's this?"

"Hand delivered, m'lord. Messenger said to tell you it is most urgent, and that the originator proposes to call on you this afternoon."

"Bloody hell." Soames quietly left the room, and Merry sank back into his pillows, eyes closed. Finally, he roused himself to put two lumps of sugar, milk, and tea into the cup. After a few sips, he let his mind relax.

He opened the envelope to see the back pages of glossy photographs. He turned the first one over and stared at the picture. He felt a cold wave of anger wash over him and sat bolt upright, upsetting the tray, and spilling the tea.

"Bloody cheek! Bloody, bloody cheek." At this point, Soames entered with the concoction that experience had shown helped his lordship recover quickest.

"Who delivered this?"

"An Asian gentleman, my lord, not one of the delivery companies."

Did he mention who sent it?"

"No, my lord. He did say his principal would call on you this afternoon. I mentioned that it might not be convenient, and if he would wait, I will confirm with your lordship. He declined to wait and said he was sure your lordship would make it convenient."

"Yes, he was right. I will see this principal. I don't suppose he had the decency to set a time, did he? Damn cheeky of these people, always taking for granted we should wait at their convenience. Anyway, please clear the afternoon for me."

"I believe the gentleman mentioned two in the afternoon."

"Damned impertinence. But yes, I'll have to be here. Oh! I'm going to the library to get out of your way."

"Thank you, my lord! Shall I bring more tea or medicine?"

"That will not be necessary, and I do not wish to be disturbed for the next hour."

"Yes, my Lord."

Once securely behind the locked door in the library, Merry sat down and looked at the album of photographs. The first one showed himself and Song in the early stages of undress and kissing passionately. The remainder of the photos depicted different stages of the progression of their encounter.

He remembered coming home from the club. He was most definitely drunk, but as he flagged a taxi, he lost his balance. A good Samaritan saved him from an embarrassing fall and possible injury. The man had helped Merry into the taxi and giving instructions to the driver, climbed in with him.

"Please accept my help in ensuring your safety, sir." Merry had accepted with a slurred "thanks."

Once he arrived home, Merry fumbled while opening the front door but managed to look closely at his saviour and saw a very handsome young Thai man.

"I say, fancy meeting you. I appreciate your help. Would have fallen otherwise. What's your name?"

"My name is Song."

Merry looked him over carefully before offering, "Look, here, you've been terribly helpful and kind. Care to come in for a drink?"

"You are most kind. That would be very welcome."

Once inside, Merry excused himself to change clothes but suggested Song use the bar and prepare something for both.

Ten minutes later, Merry returned in his dressing gown to find Song standing at the bar clad only in a pair of startlingly white briefs. *What is this?* But Merry's drunken state did not allow him to dwell on the question, and his jaw dropped as another part of his anatomy rose spectacularly.

Song grinned and, grasping Merry behind the head and the waist, pulled him close while planting a soft kiss that disclosed a hungry tongue.

The rest was history, albeit erotic, if not pornographic history, except there came the point when they had relaxed for some refreshments, after which Merry had no recollection of what happened next or how he had managed to get to bed. That could mean that Merry's drink had been spiked, maybe with

Rohipnol or something similar, to arrange to take these photographs. But why?

Photographs of erotic encounters between consenting adults in private could hardly be used for general publication, especially if the machinery of government and wealth were brought to bear. If, despite efforts to prevent publication, the gutter press somehow did manage to acquire these pictures, a considerable amount of embarrassment could ensue, but that was the extent of it.

As he went over the pictures, his annoyance was replaced by the recollection of the evening spent in unexpected and unplanned erotic intimacy. He smiled at the recollection. How, he wondered, could he arrange that again for the future?

Never-the-less, Merry did not relish the reactions of his friends and acquaintances should his encounters become known. Not that too many could take a high moral stand for themselves. No! His crime would be that he had been caught on record.

There would be sniggers and snide remarks behind his back, and he might find himself temporarily sent to Coventry socially or consigned to some meaningless tasks within the Civil Service, but all that could disappear with time.

He looked at the pictures again closely and wondered if Song set this up. "Clever, little bugger. But not too smart. Or, was this a ploy by someone else?" Perhaps Cheng was telling him, in a not-too-subtle

manner, that Merry was expected to deliver as requested. "No, Mr. Bloody Cheng, you won't get the
cooperation you want from me." With that, he locked
the photographs in his safe and went out to get
dressed and start the rest of the day.

As expected, Soames announced the visitor
was waiting in the library on time. Merry entered expecting to see Cheng Fu or maybe even Song. Instead, he was met by a middle-aged Asian in a well-
fitting suit, turning from the window to greet him.

"Viscount Hantington! So good of you to receive
me."
"Good afternoon. Mr.… ?"

"My name is of no importance."

"I see, old boy; in that case, this meeting cannot
be important, and I bid you a good afternoon." He
moved to summon Soames but stopped when his
visitor quietly interjected.

"We both know that is not quite true."

"We do, do we?"

"As I am sure you recognize, those pictures
could cause some embarrassment and gossip, both
of which I feel you would prefer to avoid." Merry
stopped and turned.

"Yes, that I can understand. And so, the purpose
of these pictures is what?"

"My superior asks you to reconsider the agreement you refused with a gentleman at your club."

"I see no reason to do so." Merry felt a rising cold anger, which he was about to express when his visitor went on.

"Mr. Cheng will honour his promise and now offers a further incentive." He looked at Merry. "An increase in the amount offered. That could be a lump sum and an all-expense paid holiday with the boy you recently met if you wish."

Merry was at a loss. *What harm could it do if I delay my responsibilities for a fun holiday? Holroyd hasn't gotten back to me, so nothing will likely happen until he does.* He let his carnal desires get the upper hand.

"Tell Mr. Cheng I will leave for a holiday in the North by the end of the week as long as I receive the money and the boy comes with me," he promised. *I can always stop it short when I hear back from Holroyd and can make contact with Beijing.*

Chapter 13

Tranh Hong worried because his work visa had expired, and he could be arrested and deported if the police stopped him. He did not wish to return to Viet Nam, even if he had the money. He had barely escaped from Saigon, or Ho Chi Min as it was now called, fearing that the police were after him. But he admitted to himself he had been lucky.

He had arrived at the house where he was to meet his section head only to see the police conducting a raid there. His boss was being manhandled out of the building with a bloodied head, and several others of the gang were already in police vehicles.

He stood there aghast at what he saw. *Are the police cracking down again or has the Serpent Triad organized this? Either way, I had better not hang around.*

Tranh was small and wiry, almost emaciated with the dark skin of a farmer. His face was wrinkled, framed by long, black, greasy hair, and he was missing two front teeth due to a barroom brawl some months earlier.

Looking at his face was not a pleasant experience, as shiftiness and even malevolence could be detected in his eyes. He had lost the little finger on his left hand as a reminder to obey and not ask questions.

Now he had a problem. Luckily, he had already been given a fake passport complete with the appropriate visa, a ticket, a sum of money, and a packet for delivery at his destination. But could he still rely on the arrangements made before the raid? Would his contact still be available, or would he have been rounded up as part of a coordinated cross-border swoop? Even if not arrested, his contact might want to lie low until matters had cooled off.

With no other choices coming to mind, he took his booked flight and, on arrival, registered in a small cheap lodging house near the waterfront.

Once in his room, Tranh phoned a number he had been given and, upon identifying himself with the appropriate codes, was told to wait. The phone rang an hour later.

A distorted voice asked, "You have the package?"

"Yes."

"Wait there. We will get back to you with instructions." Not long after that, the phone rang again, and he was told to go to an address where he was to deliver the package and receive new instructions.

On arrival at the address, Tranh was searched, the package removed, and he was told to wait with two burly guards watching over him. Some thirty minutes later, he was escorted into a room where he faced three men.

"You cannot go back. The police are all over our organization there. Instead, we are planning for you to deliver another package somewhere else. That package and the travel arrangements will be delivered to you shortly. Until then, stay in your lodgings and keep a low profile." With that, he was dismissed.

He received the package and two envelopes. One contained an airline ticket to Panama City and papers, stating he was a cruise ship crew member. He was on his way to rejoin his ship in Panama. The call came soon after.

"Confirm you have received everything," he was asked. "Good! Another of our organization will meet and take care of you once out of the Airport at your destination. He has been told to watch out for your arrival and has been given the necessary information to recognise and approach you. You will replace a crewman who is also called Tranh."

"But won't the other crew members know I have taken this Tranh's place?"

"Most of the crew is white and have difficulty identifying one Asian from another. But if anyone raises the matter he would regret it.

"The ship is on a cruise from Miami to San Diego and will stop in Panama and Acapulco. In Panama, more parcels will be brought on board. You will be told exactly how to identify and then hide those parcels among the ship's normal stores," he stopped, "Do you understand those instructions?"

"Yes," Tranh said, "what happens then?"

"The ship will take you to Acapulco in Mexico," he was told, " Once there, you will make sure the consignment is unloaded, and leave the ship to go to an address we will give you when you are ready."

"Won't they come looking for me if I don't return to the ship? "Tranh asked.

"Not immediately," the voice replied. "Crewmen sometimes get drunk ashore and miss the ship's departure. By the time anyone realises you have jumped ship, you will be long gone."

***

In Beijing, Wen Mei Li answered the phone. "Wei?" and her anonymous informer reported that a courier was on his way to Mexico with a sizeable product parcel.

She acknowledged the report and then asked, "This is not the usual way for you to report. Why are you informing me of this transfer? "

"The travel arrangements appear to be novel. The courier will fly to Panama with a temporary visa that will permit him to join a ship there as a member of the crew."

"Do we know which ship?"

"Not yet."

"Keep me informed when you have more news," she instructed. "Meanwhile, follow the normal procedures for such cases." She cut the connection and sat back, thinking. *As far as I know, we don't have anyone down there, and I don't want to draw attention to myself by asking around. I know Peter is there, but I can't involve him. Perhaps Meredith can help.*

Picking up her cell phone, she dialled a number that Merry had given her, only to get a voicemail answer. She left a message for Merry to call her back as soon as he could.

***

Unable to get a reply from Sean, Holroyd called Merry and left a message to express his worry at being unable to make contact. He asked Merry to make some enquiries through the diplomatic channels.

Chapter 14

"I think I may have found where the stele is," Philip announced.

"Or was," Holroyd interrupted. "We won't know if it's still there until we go look over the place." Philip ignored the interruption and continued. "It's down the coast, but there's no convenient land access."

"That's very promising," Holroyd said. "It means it was probably put up by sailors and that would prove my theory." He paused. "Let's go!"

"When you stop interrupting, I'll finish by telling you what I've organised," Philip said reprovingly.

Holroyd assumed a contrite look and Philip went on.

"A couple of my flock are fishermen and have agreed to take us there and back. I promised we would pay them." He stopped. "I take it that is correct?"

Holroyd nodded. Philip ended his report by saying, "We leave before sunrise so that we won't be out on the water at noon. In any case, bring sunscreen and some clothing for protection."

Both men retired early but got up to get to the harbour on time. The sun would rise in an hour, but the night was still dark with a heavy overcast.

Holroyd stood listening to the sounds of seagulls squabbling over scraps of food that littered the dock, the growl of boats' engines as fishermen arrived with their morning catches, and the lapping of waves against the pier.

Men were busy on the dock, unloading their catches and shouting at each other, although Holroyd didn't understand what they were saying. He took a deep breath, savouring the smells of salt in the air and of fish that had been landed.

A morning wind gusted to ruffle the waters and there were occasional whitecaps, but Holroyd with his Naval experience was not worried. He had lived through Atlantic storms at sea and the sea here was almost smooth by comparison.

They were welcomed by two men, father and son as Holroyd learned, and clambered on board the wooden fishing smack. They cast off immediately and chugged out to join dozens of other boats putting out to sea.

Excited by the prospect of finally proving the Chinese had been the first foreigners to the Americas, Holroyd settled on a hatch cover and prepared to enjoy the outing.

***

The cruise ship **Distant Horizons,** slowed as she entered Acapulco. The master stood next to the control panel and surveyed the harbour entrance where the city's bright lights could be seen ahead.

Reaching for the bridge binoculars, the master swept the seas ahead. Ahead, he could see the flashing lights of navigational markers and many small lights denoting local fishing boats. Glancing at the ship's head, he satisfied himself that there was no immediate danger of a collision and moved to the radar console. Immediately, he noted significant clutter, signifying a mix of sea clutter and small pleasure or fishing boats. *Well, the early fisherman gets the catch or something like that.*

Plotting his position and course, the master ensured the ship was not approaching any dangers. Forethought was necessary because the Distant Horizon was slow in responding to helm and engine changes. Any avoiding action needed to be initiated at least a mile or two away from impact and more if the collision was with an approaching vessel. Once again, the master swept the seas ahead to ensure nothing had changed.

Noting nothing out of the ordinary, the master relaxed, feeling secure that the local pilot on board would give warning of any potential traffic problems. Nevertheless, good lookouts were essential, and the master satisfied himself that the Watch was in place and hopefully alert.

"Keep a good lookout!" the master ordered the bridge crew. "These are dangerous waters!" The two bridge lookouts acknowledged the order. Satisfied the watch was as ready as they could be, the master turned to the officer behind him and said, "Alert the crew to prepare for coming alongside, Mister Mate."

"Yes, Captain."

"Looks good," he muttered and turned towards the back of the bridge where a coffee maker was perking a fresh brew. He glanced at his two bridge lookouts to make sure they were scanning their respective sectors and turned back to pour a mug of the aromatic brew and add sugar. The ship would be alongside in about an hour.

***

Holroyd realised the boat's engine had stopped, and he could hear the son below trying to get it re-started. *Damn! Just what I need! Another block to my getting to the stele.* He was just about to ask how long it would be before they could get underway when Philip sitting in the bow let out a yell.

Holroyd twisted to see what was wrong and saw a huge black shape with a large white bow wave bearing down on them. There was a hefty splintering crash, and he found himself in the warm waters. When he surfaced, he saw the ship had not stopped.

He yelled, but the wind and the sea tore his cry away, and the ship continued on its way, leaving any survivors to their fates. *Those careless bastards! leaving us to swim in the drink after running us down...I wonder if I can swim to shore or perhaps over to one of the fishing boats... Can Philip swim?....what of the others in the crew? ...Is anyone wounded?.... Is there any wreckage that can provide support, perhaps even out of the water?*

With thoughts spinning in his mind, Holroyd started swimming, looking among the boat's wreckage for the other members of his boat's crew. He found Philip floating unconscious but luckily face up, but of the other crew members, he could see nothing. Towing Philip to the boat's remains, he noticed another boat approaching and managed to hail them.

***

On board the ship, the master noticed a slight jolt and looked around but could see nothing that was nearby, but perhaps the ship had struck flotsam that was ever-present in these waters. Any collision could dent or even breach the hull if it happened at speed, but because the ship's speed was slow and the jar caused only a slight tremor, the master was satisfied it was probably not the case.

A quick look at the chart on a table at the back of the bridge and the depth sounders indicated no rocks or shoals in this position. Of more immediate concern was the possibility that whatever it was could get tangled in the ship's stabilizers, rudder, or propellers, and he immediately ordered: "Stop engines. Get the engineers to check for damage."

"The Engine room reports no damage, Captain. We can proceed."

Satisfied, the master continued with the process of entering the port. The only sounds came from the bridge's electronic equipment and some entertainment below decks. This would be the last visit of the cruise before returning to home port, and from experience, he knew the passengers would go ashore and eagerly enjoy what the city had to offer.

Once the ship was safely alongside, the master watched as the port authorities came on board to complete the formalities for entering the port. He waited for the party to come to the bridge. However, this time the harbour master was accompanied by an officer from the Mexican Coast Guard and police officers, but from which jurisdiction he could not recognize.

"Good morning, Capitan."

"Good morning, gentlemen. Is there a problem?"

"A fisherman reported your ship was in a collision on entering port," the harbour master said, "is there anything you can tell us?"

"I'm not aware of such a collision, but we did touch some flotsam."

"Can you show us where this happened?"

The master led the delegation to the chart with the ship's route. He then consulted the ship's logs before pointing to a position.

"About here."

"*Si!* That confirms our reports," the harbour master confirmed.

"Well, Capitan. I regret to inform you that you did not touch any flotsam, but you ran down a fishing vessel with four on board," the Coast Guard officer stated and waited before continuing. "As fatalities are involved, your ship will not be allowed to leave port while there are ongoing investigations."

"What about the passengers?" the master protested. "They are eager to go ashore. What can I tell them?"

"Everyone will remain on board until our investigations are complete," the officer replied.

"They will not be happy, and the owners will go berserk," the master remarked. "There goes my bonus pay."

The officer just shrugged, and the delegation left the ship.

***

Once ashore, Philip was rushed to hospital, but Holroyd was allowed to go home.

Sitting alone, Holroyd went over the incident. *I can't imagine we were intentionally run down, in which was a case of error or carelessness. What it achieved is injuries to Philip that may be life-*

threatening. Another thought occurred to him. *If Philip does not recover, I will have to start from scratch in my search for the stele, and I don't know whom to approach.*

Chapter 15

After Holroyd visited Philip in hospital, he decided to go visit Strang and see what interests in transpacific trade he wanted to discuss.

Remembering his experience with American spooks in China who had tried to interfere with his task at the time[9], he was wary of any contacts with American law enforcement agencies. *Given Mickie told me he is a resident spook, I think he was referring to the movement of drugs. If so, will he be helpful or a hindrance?* He decided he had better find out.

Looking through his pockets, he found the business card Strang had given him. Holroyd commandeered a taxi that stopped to discharge another visitor to the hospital.

His destination was an imposing building among high-end shops on Acapulco's main shopping boulevard. *I'd have thought it rather ostentatious to have an office here, but then, Americans tend to be flashy.* The receptionist in the lobby directed him to the fifth floor.

Exiting the lift, he faced glass double doors that opened automatically to let him enter. A pretty receptionist sat behind a desk flanked on one side by an American Flag and on the other, by a blue flag that Holroyd did not recognize. On the wall between the

---

[9] The Dragon's Threat

flags was a photograph of President Trump that Holroyd tried to ignore. The receptionist looked up as he approached the desk.

"*Si, señor,*" she greeted him ."*¿Como puedo ayudarte?*"

"I'm sorry," he said sheepishly. "I don't speak Spanish."

"Oh, then how may I be of assistance?"

"I'm here to meet Mr. Strang."

"Do you have an appointment?"

"No."

"May I know your name and let me see if he is available." She ducked down to phone someone.

"Mr. Strang will see you," she reported before picking up the phone again. That done, she asked Holroyd to wait a moment before Marie-José would accompany him to Mr. Strang's office.

Marie-José was a beautiful indigenous woman who did not speak English but led him through corridors and past offices with people busy on computers, reading files, or in meetings. *This is a very large organization, and Strang must be very senior if he is the head of it.*

He was.

After coffee was served and the social preliminaries concluded, Strang came straight to the point.

"Well, Professor. Why are you here?" he asked, "And don't give me any bullshit about looking for ancient Chinese monuments. There aren't any." He stopped, waiting for Holroyd to respond. Holroyd said nothing.

"Ok, just to be clear, I also don't buy your story about going sunbathing," Strang went on. "Unless there's an emergency, no one travels halfway round the world to go to the beach in one of the most dangerous parts of the Earth. So why are you really here?"

"You know, Mr. Strang, I find your tone offensive," Holroyd said, his eyes narrowed to a pair of slits, "you invited me to drop in to discuss common interests and start doubting why I am here."

"Don't pretend to be innocent," Strang seized the initiative again. "I know all about you from your China activities, and that reporter, Mickie, brought some more information to me. You most definitely are not the meek academic you pretend to be."

Holroyd was utterly taken by surprise and became furious. *What has Mickie been telling him?* Controlling his emotions, he looked coldly at Strang. "How dare you accuse me of deceit, Mr. Strang," he said icily.

Strang sat up. "Watch it, buddy," he warned. "Don't go there."

But Holroyd ignored the warning. "I don't think you are what your business card says you are," he continued. "Furthermore, I think you asked me here on false pretences. I don't think there are common interests we could discuss. So, who is pretending here?"

Strang looked at Holroyd before leaning forward.

"I'm the one who's asking the questions here and, in case it hasn't sunk in on you, I'm doing so in my official capacity." He let Holroyd think about that and then continued, "I have many duties here, one of which is to monitor the movement of drugs from China." He again let Holroyd think before continuing. "When you arrive here with your background and with a story that to say the least, is different, I take notice."

"You mean you suspect I might be involved in the drug trade," observed Holroyd.

"Yes."

"You give me too much credit. The closest I've come to that is when my teenage son tried mariju-ana."

"I doubt that very much," Strang said dis-missively, "and as long as you are in my neck of the woods, and until I'm convinced you're clean, be very careful where you go and who you meet."

Holroyd sat shocked, unable to respond as Strang stood up and gathered some papers from his desk.

"We're done here, Professor. Now, if you will excuse me, I have a meeting to go to. Marie-José will show you out."

Holroyd stood up and was about to make a cutting comment to show his outrage at how he had been treated but decided that discretion would be the better part of valour. *Alright, Mr. High and Mighty Strang. I'm sure we will be in contact again, and then let's see who laughs last.*

Chapter 16

 Tranh leant against the ship's rail and looked at the port activity below. He noticed two soldiers or maybe police officers had been posted at the gangway and no one had been allowed to leave the ship. *Is this a normal delay or is something wrong?* He decided to find someone who could tell him what was happening. As he went down to the gangway deck the public announcement system came alive.

"Attention, please. Ladies and Gentlemen, we have encountered a small problem which will delay disembarking for the moment. You will be advised when you can go ashore." The announcement was repeated in Spanish and French.

Tranh turned around and went up to his berth. Once there, he called a number he had been given and reported the problem.

"Have you been given a time when you can go ashore?"

"No," Tranh answered.

"Let us know when you can." The line went dead.

Tranh stayed in his berth until he saw several uniformed men approaching. Wanting to avoid any contact with whoever these men represented, he started to get away.

"*Hola, hombre. detente.*" Tranh gave no sign of having heard and made as if to continue.

"Hey! I said stop," the officer repeated but more forcefully. This time, Tranh, knowing he could only delay but not escape capture, stopped.

"Come here," the officer commanded, and Tranh resignedly shuffled over to where the officers were standing.

"Is this your berth?" the officer asked. Tranh nodded and the officer then asked, "Do you share this with anyone?" and Tranh shook his head. The officer nodded and ordered one of the officers accompanying him to start searching.

"What is this?" Tranh started to protest. "You have no right to search here."

"*Teniente, nosotras encontramos el paquete aqui,*" and the searching officer held up one of the parcels that Tranh had been told to deliver.

"You see?" the Lieutenant grinned at Tranh. "We have every right to search." He turned back to the officer holding the parcel. "*ábrelo.*"

The parcel was opened to reveal several wrapped packets, one of which was cut open to reveal a white powder.

"Is this your package?" Tranh said nothing.

"I know there are more parcels, so where are they?" The officer looked at Tranh as a butcher might consider a side of beef before starting to cut. Tranh remained silent.

The officer nodded and turned to give one of his men an order.

"I have just ordered a complete search of this ship," he informed Tranh, "and don't think we won't find it. This ship is going nowhere, and no one leaves the ship until we do." He stopped. "Meanwhile, you are under arrest for importing illegal drugs into Mexico," and Tranh was handcuffed and with his belongings taken off the ship.

"How did you know to look for me?" Tranh asked petulantly.

"We have friends," grinned the Lieutenant.

Tranh was annoyed but not afraid of what could happen. He knew his organization controlled almost all the prisons in Mexico. He would be safe enough. He knew there would be swift retribution once he discovered how he had been betrayed and passed on the information. He could expect to be free very soon.

***

"Juanita! Get Jimenez in here now!" Acapulco's Chief of police was not in a good mood. "And I don't care where he is or what he's doing; get him here now, or you'll be out on the street."

Juanita fled and was lucky to find the Lieutenant in the corridor outside the Chief's Office. He was a large man, overweight, bald, and bursting out of his uniform but possessed high intelligence and a sense of honour that few knew about. Those of his colleagues who knew him well made sure to remain on his good side, whereas anyone who failed to do so would quickly realise their error as they found themselves assigned to the least pleasant duties.

"The *Jefe* wants you. And he wants you now," she blurted out breathlessly.

Jimenez looked at the girl, nodded and went straight to the chief's office. He found the chief dressed impeccably in his uniform, standing in front of the room's large window, and staring at the scene outside.

"*Teniente*," the chief spoke softly. "Come here and tell me what you see."

Jimenez went over to stand by the chief and looked outside. "I see the harbour *Jefe*," he said, "with a couple of ships. Over there, I see buildings, the tops of trees, and some boats out to sea."

"And what strikes you as unusual?"

Jimenez looked carefully at the scene, but before he could say anything, the chief continued, "I see a cruise ship that should no longer be there. Why is that?"

"It's being held until we can complete our enquiries into the collision that killed a couple of local fishermen."

"I am given to understand the collision took place because the victims' boat failed to get out of the cruise ship's path. That being so, why is the ship being held?"

"We arrested a drug smuggler and confiscated some drugs. But there are more drugs on board, and we are conducting a search of the whole ship looking for them."

"Was the smuggler on board or ashore?"

"On board."

"Have any drugs been landed here from that ship?"

"No."

"Then why is the ship still here?"

"*Jefe*? What are you saying?" Jimenez was puzzled.

"I received several calls from Mexico City. The Minister wants to know on what authority the ship is still here," the chief stated, "and the President's

Office called to tell me the Americans are furious at what they call a highhanded and unauthorized action."

"But *Jefe*..."Jimenez got no further.

"Don't *Jefe* me, you fool," the chief lost it and turning to Jimenez, screamed. "Have you been drinking or are you on drugs? You incompetent idiot!" His voice rose to another level. "Have you any idea of the consequences? You, your family, every policeman here could be a target for reprisals by the gangs." He lingered to let Jimenez think about it.

He calmed down somewhat and in a tone that brooked no argument, ordered, "Release the man you arrested, return to him his belongings whatever they are, and inform the captain of the ship he may leave at his convenience." He took a deep breath before continuing, "and you take some leave until I call you back."

Jimenez marched out of the office as quickly as he could. Once outside, he called his trusted men and ordered them to go to the docks and inform the master and the harbourmaster that the ship was free to leave.

"What about the prisoner?"

"Oh!" Jimenez said, looking at the sky, "What a shame he missed the ship. Find him accommodation that only we know about and where we can talk to him without fear of being overheard."

The men grinned, nodded their understanding, and left to carry out their instructions.

***

Tranh proved to be obstinate under interrogation, but his interrogators were experienced, ruthless, and patient. Finally, Tranh broke down and confessed he was under the orders of an organization in Vietnam. The organization was headed by a Chinese man, but Tranh did not know the man's name or where he could be found.

The information was passed on to Jimenez, who tried to contact Merry. When that failed, he called Holroyd and passed on the information. Holroyd tried to reach Merry, but when that failed, he called Wen Mei Li and was able to pass on what he had been told.

Chapter 17

Holroyd considered what his next step should be. Philip was not expected to be released for a couple more days, and the beaches didn't hold quite the same allure as tourist brochures suggested. He decided to go to the cantina for refreshment but would borrow a book from Philip's library to occupy his time.

Philip's library was stocked with many books, but on inspection, Holroyd discovered almost all were focused on religious themes, social problem discussions, and economic theories. *It's not really what I'd like to read right now, or ever, for that matter.* "Nothing I really want to read," he groaned, "and I don't remember seeing where I can get an English newspaper."

His search was interrupted by the phone. He debated whether he should answer it and thought it might be the hospital with news of Philip.

"Mr. Holroyd, meet me in the cantina you and Brother Philip go to," a heavily accented voice ordered, "I shall come up to you, and you will greet me as an old and good friend you have not seen for many years." The line went dead. *What the hell? I have no idea who this is, but I suppose I'll be safe in a public space.*

Arriving at the cantina, Holroyd chose a table near the wall, ordered a coffee, and pretended to study the menu. Several people were sitting at other tables, and there was a steady stream of new clients coming in. Some of the arrivals looked at him, but none approached him. Finally, he gave up the pretense of further study and ordered a burrito. As he took his first bite, three policemen came in.

Maria greeted the newcomers cheerfully and Holroyd understood this was a common occurrence from the exchanges that followed. Then he noticed Maria pointing at him and one of the officers, a Lieutenant by his insignia, came over with a huge smile on his face.

Holroyd stood up to greet the man. *Who is this man and why would a lieutenant want to meet with me?* Remembering Philip's warning about who might be listening, he waited for the approaching man to make the first move.

"Peter!" he said in a loud voice. "What are you doing here?" and Holroyd was enveloped in a big hug.

"Maria, two Coronas, please." The Lieutenant sat down opposite Holroyd. "Let me introduce myself. I am Jose Maria Jimenez, and I have been expecting you for some time," he said in a low voice as if to avoid being overheard.

Miguel brought the beers over together with some nachos and guacamole but seemed reluctant to return to his other duties, suggesting he wanted to listen to the conversation. Jimenez noticed it and ordered the man to leave.

Giving a surly look at the Lieutenant, Miguel shuffled off towards the kitchen but then stopped and turned. Holroyd saw Miguel reach under his apron when a shot rang out, and with a surprised look on his face, Miguel collapsed on the floor, and a pistol slid out from his lifeless hand.

Chaos ensued as patrons reacted with screams or shouts to the shot, some running towards the door, others trying to hide under their table. Maria stood beside the bar with her hand over her mouth, looking as if trying to quell a rising hysteria.

Holroyd was shocked and stared at the corpse as Jimenez got up to survey the scene. One of his men was standing with a pistol in his hand, facing toward where Miguel had fallen.

"*Ese hombre te iba a disparar,*" he said before switching to English. "He was going to shoot you."

"Me?" asked Holroyd, still dazed.

"No! I was the target," observed Jimenez. He gave his men some orders before turning back to Holroyd.

"As you can see, Peter, Acapulco is not safe," he said. "However, you and I have some matters to discuss that are important to our mutual friend, Meredith. I will contact you to set up a less exciting place to continue our discussions, but for now, I suggest you leave."

"I need a stiff drink before I go anywhere," replied Holroyd. Jimenez looked at him and turned to Maria.

"*Tráenos una bebida fuerte, querida.*" Maria nodded and brought over a glass of colourless liquid that Holroyd swallowed in one gulp, gasped, and coughed as the liquid went into his stomach. Finally, he got up.

"Thank you, Maria. Lieutenant, I will go home to recover," he said, "You know where I can be found."

Still shaken, Holroyd managed to get home to collapse on the couch. *This does it, Merry! Once again, you have landed me in a swamp filled with alligators and snakes. But this time, I'm not going to take it lying down.*

Chapter 18

The front doorbell rang, and Holroyd went to answer it, only to be faced by a young boy neatly dressed in an open-necked shirt and short pants.

"*Mi padre te pide por favor ven conmigo,*" he said.

"I don't speak Spanish, young man," he looked at the boy.

"*Ah, si,*" the boy replied, "please come."

"No," Holroyd said, "I don't know who you are or why I should trust you enough to go with you."

The boy understood because he pulled Holroyd out from the door and pointed down the street where a police car was parked. As he stood looking at it, one of the policemen came out of the car and waved. Holroyd recognised him as the one who had shot Miguel.

Reassured this summons was not a trap, Holroyd nodded and shut the door behind him before walking over to the car with the boy. Once seated, the car sped off.

"Where are we going?" Holroyd asked not expecting he would be understood or that he would be answered.

"To the family house of Teniente Jimenez," the driver replied in good English. "You have been invited to dinner. Oh! The boy is the family's oldest son."

"*Me llamo Martin*," the boy announced proudly, smiling at Holroyd.

"Hello, Martin," Holroyd smiled back. "Nice to meet you."

Jimenez's home proved to be a two-story house with a flat roof set back behind a low wall. Holroyd was led inside and welcomed by the family but noted that the police car remained parked outside.

Jimenez's wife was a cheerful and diminutive but comfortably padded lady who grabbed him by the hand and led him through to the patio. There, a table laden with Mexican dishes and bottles of fruit juices, beer and wine was set out and four other children were introduced.

The children whispered and giggled among themselves, shyly casting curious eyes on Holroyd. The conversation went smoothly, with Jimenez alternating between translator and *pater familias*.

When dinner was over, the children went to their rooms except for Martin, who was sent to the roof to keep watch. Jimenez dismissed the police car and led Holroyd into the library, where he closed the door and the curtains. They settled into comfortable armchairs, and Jimenez began talking.

"I try to help in the fight against drugs," he started. "It's not easy as I will explain but let me just say I pass on to Meredith in London information that sometimes comes to my attention. But of late, less information has been coming, and I discovered several of my sources have disappeared or turned up dead."

He stopped before continuing, "I think there is a traitor among the policemen here. If I raise the matter officially, I or my family is likely to be punished in a very unpleasant manner."

Holroyd said nothing.

"What do you know of the drug situation we have here in Mexico?"

"Only what I have read in the press," Holroyd admitted, "but it's not something I follow closely."

"Historically, cocaine has been the drug most associated with Latin American cartels, but now organized crime groups, including Mexican drug cartels, are mainly producing and trafficking synthetic drugs such as methamphetamine and fentanyl," Jimenez started. "With access to modern communications and modes of transportation, Mexican cartels and, of course, others, have established trans-pacific partnerships that are responsible for much of the drug trade entering the United States." He paused to light a cigarette before continuing, "and, of course to Europe." He inhaled, savouring the smoke entering his lungs.

"But the biggest threat comes from how these cartels operate here within Mexico. One cartel gained notoriety for a series of attacks on security forces and public officials. It downed an army helicopter with a rocket-propelled grenade, killed dozens of state officials, and has even been known to hang the bodies of its victims from bridges to intimidate its rivals and possible informers.

"The gangs recruit children, use prisons and street gangs as hubs for crime, destroy neighbourhoods by intergang feuds, and engage in mass killings." He stopped to light another cigarette.

"Eventually, the government lost control of its penal system, with prisoners coercing other prisoners into paying for beds, services and security, and even holding the keys to their own prison blocks. Penitentiaries became operating bases for the drug trade.

"Television news stations are regularly filled with stories of beheadings, car bombs, police assassinations, young men hanging from bridges, and children gunned down outside their homes or schools. More recently, gangs have found another source of income: extortion. Shopkeepers, community leaders, even water providers, trash collectors and schools are forced to pay a tax to criminal groups in exchange for their safety. As one community leader reported, "We are threatened. You don't want to join? We will kill your family."

He stopped to light another cigarette.

"It's not just the cartels who play a part in this scenario. Peasants, far from being the feeble lackeys of powerful traffickers, have used drug production as a tool to protect their communities from outside threats, whether from the state, capitalist development, or the traffickers themselves.

"Vigilante groups known as *autodefensas* have sought to fill in where security forces have failed to protect communities from criminal groups. They have become a formidable force against the cartels in states including Guerrero and Michoacán. However, some vigilantes have committed rights abuses, including the recruitment of child fighters; allegedly maintained ties to cartels in exchange for weapons and protection; and even turned to organized crime themselves."

"To give you an example of just how bad it is. Forty-three students from a university in Mexico's Guerrero State protesting the government's inaction in countering the power of the drug cartels were abducted and killed, though the remains of only three students have been definitively identified." He waited to let Holroyd think about that.

"Investigations into the students' disappearances have purportedly found evidence that authorities, including the police and military, conspired with cartel members in the crime." Jimenez went on.

"Oh, my goodness," Holroyd exclaimed. "That's horrible. I can't imagine the challenges you face, but you have my respect and admiration for even trying."

"My biggest problem is knowing who I can trust other than the two officers who brought you here. As it is, I worry daily for the safety of our families. And on top of it all, I am convinced I am fighting elements of the very organization that is supposed to work with and support my little group."

"Can you give examples of why you reached that conclusion?" Holroyd asked.

"The first sign was the disappearance of too many of my informants in a very short time. I expect informants to disappear from time to time, either because the gangs punish them or because they go into hiding. But the disappearances have increased so dramatically that I can only believe someone is betraying them.

"And then only this morning I was countermanded by my superior. I had impounded the cruise ship that ran you down because there was a drug runner on board carrying a large quantity of drugs to be delivered to the States. I arrested him, confiscated the drugs he had in his possession, and we were searching for more drugs." He hesitated as if considering his next statement

"Without warning, I was ordered to release the runner, return his drugs to him, and cancel the ship's detention," Jimenez said wearily.

"Ordered by whom?" Holroyd asked.

"My chief of police, but I don't think he dares to give such an order," Jimenez replied. "But he certainly doesn't have the courage to disobey whoever gave the order."

"Does Meredith know all this?"

"I think he does on a broad scale, " Jimenez answered. "He won't know about the local situation here in Acapulco. But he should be told because Acapulco is a major port of entry for Asian drugs," he stopped.

"Given the disappearances of so many of my informers, I think there is a new power in town, but I don't know who or what it is. That worries me because I have no idea where the next attack on me or my men will come from."

With that, Holroyd was taken home. Once there, he sat back, thinking over what he had learned. *I expected something else. The local American thinks I'm here in connection with the drug trade, even though I have no idea how he comes to that conclusion. Next, someone shoots at me or the person I'm having coffee with, and then I get a briefing on the local state of play. Pearl will be furious. My best course of action is to throw this back into Merry's lap. It's, after all, his game, not mine. After that, I will continue on my quest.*

He tried to contact Merry, but no one answered. Nor did anyone answer when he tried again. *That's strange. Why isn't he answering?* He suddenly realized that, as on previous occasions, he was left to his own devices but more likely hanging out to dry. *Here we go again.* Somehow, he didn't feel confident or safe. *But Merry needs to know Jimenez thinks a new player is in town.*

Chapter 19

Merry woke and stared at the ceiling while gathering his thoughts. He felt a slight movement by his side and turned to look at the still-sleeping Song.

He looked at the boy, feeling a sudden but unfamiliar tenderness, and lay there just looking at Song's head enveloped deep in a very large down pillow. After a moment, he slid out of bed, carefully not to disturb Song, put on his dressing gown, and went to the dining room.

He rang the bell to let Fiona, now his housekeeper, know he was up. As he sat at the table waiting for breakfast he looked over the newspapers already laid out for him.

Only one item caught his interest. It was a report of an American cruise ship detained in Acapulco. He read of the American outrage and the diplomatic exchanges as the Mexicans tried to diffuse the situation but without success.

The Americans were furious the ship had been detained and passengers had not been allowed ashore, but they also accused the Mexicans of releasing a reported huge shipment of illicit drugs by allowing the ship to leave for San Diego. *That's duplicitous: how can the Mexicans release a ship when it is known to be carrying drugs?*

Normally, Merry would have started phoning his people and his contacts in other agencies to get a full briefing, but not this time. *Mr. Cheng, I hope you are pleased with the service you are getting.*

He reached for his cell phone and noted that he had missed calls from Holroyd and Wen Mei Li. There were several messages from contacts in other departments, all of whom demanded to know where he was and what he proposed to do about the incident.

Fiona entered carrying the breakfast tray. As she placed tea, toast, and a plate of eggs and bacon in front of him, she asked, "Will the young man be joining ye soonest, or shall I keep his eggs and bacon warm?"

"Keep them warm, please, Fiona."

She nodded and stood there until Merry looked at her and asked, "Is there anything else?"

"Aye there is," she looked at him sternly. "Ye're nae behaving normally and I dinna like it. And I'm not the only one hae noticed it. There's talk in the village." Merry looked as if he'd been slapped across the face.

Before he could say anything, Fiona went on. "I've been with this family since you were a wee bairn. I've acted as your nursemaid and yer nanny. I ken ye all too well, Meredith, and I've accepted your behaviour both because it's not my affair and it never hurt anyone. But I think ye're going too far this time. It's time for that young man tae leave and for you tae get back tae work." She left the dining room.

Merry sat gathering his thoughts. *She's right of course, but if only it were that simple. I must think what Cheng will do if I tell Song to leave. At the same time, I don't want Song to go, and I will have to decide what to do with him.*

He looked at his cell phone, wondering if he could do an end run on Cheng by calling Wen Mei Li or trying to get an update from Holroyd. *I can't call my office because that will launch a whole set of problems, not the least of which will be when I come back to work.* He heard Song coming down and greeting Fiona.

Song entered wearing one of Merry's dressing gowns and, after planting a kiss on Merry's cheek, sat down as Fiona came in with his breakfast.

"There's a phone call for you," Fiona announced. "It's yer ma."

"Can you tell I'll call back?"

"Not this time, laddie." Fiona looked at him. "It's serious."

Merry got up with a sigh and went to take the call. Fiona looked at Song.

"If ye hae a shred of decency in ye," she spoke sternly, "Ye'd leave now before ye cause any mair problems." Song looked up at her with fright and despair, but before he could say anything Merry returned.

"My father has died," he said tonelessly. "I have to go home."

"Och no!" Fiona groaned "Ye puir man. I am sae sorry."

"I am sorry too, Merry," Song added, getting up and preparing to hug Merry.

"Don't you dare touch His Lordship in that way, young man," Fiona warned. "He is now the Duke of Rannoalgh and Earl of the Inner and Outer Isles. As such, he gets a lot more respect than you've been giving him."

"No, Fiona," Merry said. "I've decided Song will come home with me." Fiona looked as if a thunderbolt had hit her.

"Are ye daft, Merry?" Shocked, Fiona cast all formality aside. "Yer ma will hae a fit."

"She may well have one," Merry replied. "But the situation has changed, and I am now Master of the House. If mother doesn't like it, I'll pension her off. Maybe send her to a convent or something like that."

"Ye wouldna dare!"

"Fiona! Don't interfere. You are a valued part of my family but do not pretend you are irreplaceable. And before you say anything more, I think Song can decide if he wants to join the family."

Fiona gasped and ran out of the room.

"Merry, what are you saying?" asked Song.

"I think you heard what I said," Merry replied. "We will discuss the matter again, but you will come with me for now. Now go get dressed. I have some matters to attend to." *Like telling Mr. Cheng the deal is off.*

***

Merry and Song arrived at the ancestral home to be greeted by the staff with a mix of condolences and newfound deference. *I will have to get comfortable with being addressed as Your Grace.* Merry took Song by the hand as their bags were taken in and went to the living room to meet with his mother.

His mother, dressed in widow's weeds, sat with an old friend but looked up as the men entered.

"Well, it's about time you arrived." She greeted him and then realised Merry was not alone. She looked carefully at Song, almost as if she were inspecting a thoroughbred horse, before asking, "Who is this person?"

"Mother, this is Song. He will be staying here."

"I will not have such a person in my house," she said. "Especially not at this time. Tell him to go away."

"Mother, this is no longer your house," Merry chided. "It's mine. You are now the Dowager Duchess and as such will respect my decisions."

His mother suddenly burst into tears and before Merry could react, Song went over to her, sat down, took her hand, and started to talk softly to her. She flinched, trying to take her hand away, but Song did not let go and continued to talk softly to her. Suddenly, his mother nestled up to Song and slowly regained her composure. There was silence in the room until Merry said.

"I think that settles it." His mother nodded, not letting go of Song's hand.

"Right, then," Merry said brusquely, "Song, please stay with mother. I have some urgent business I must attend to."

Merry went to the study and started making calls. He called his office to set up a briefing, left a message with the Cabinet Secretary to say he was back and would like to discuss his immediate future, and tried without success to reach either Holroyd or Wen Mei Li.

"It's time to clean house," he muttered, "and I'm wielding the broom this time."

Chapter 20

Holroyd realized the value of the information he had been given by Jimenez and tried to call Merry but was unable to get through.

He decided to visit Strang; even though he disliked the man, he acknowledged his role as the American local representative. After some delay, he was ushered into Strang's office.

"Well?" Strang asked, but Holroyd thought the question was more for form's sake rather than interest in what Holroyd might have to say.

"I have some information and thought you might be interested," Holroyd answered and gave a short summary of what Jimenez had told him. Strang listened and then asked.

"And who gave you all this information?"

"I think I will first ask whether I can pass on the informant's identity," Holroyd hedged.

"Let me get this straight," Strang leaned forward. "You come in here with a story that implicates the police chief, and you won't tell me where you got the information?"

Holroyd nodded.

"I don't believe you," Strang sat back. "What I can believe is that you dreamed up this story to discredit the chief, who, in my experience, is doing a really good job."

"What?" Holroyd started, but Strang hadn't finished.

"I ask myself, why would Professor Holroyd dream up such a story?" Strang paused. "Obviously, because his buddies know the police are closing in on them. So, they look for and get a convenient puppet to run interference. Your strings have been pulled, pal."

"Are you out of your mind?" Holroyd demanded.

"Nope," Strang dismissed the question. "You may be, and if so, be very careful with whom you share your wet dream."

"Believe me, it's not a dream," Holroyd countered. "And as for sharing it, I know exactly whom to call."

"And just who might that be?"

"You have no reason to know that." Holroyd stood up. "I'll see myself out."

Strang waited until Holroyd was out of the office and picked up his phone.

"Put a tap on Holroyd's phone," he instructed.

                              ***

As he stepped out into the street, Holroyd heard his name. Turning to see who was calling, he saw Mickie coming down the street.

"Hi, Professor," she greeted him and then looked at the door from which he had just come out. "What did the resident spook have to say?"

"Nothing new," Holroyd answered shortly. "Have a good day, Mickie." And he walked away. *This woman is beginning to annoy me. I think it's time to lose her.*

                              ***

Mickie watched him go. *Something smells. Let's see if I can find out what.* Impulsively she decided to visit Strang. She caught him as he was walking down the corridor with a file under his arm.

"Hey Mickie," Strang greeted her. "How's it going?"

"I just saw Holroyd come out of here," she replied. "Can you tell me why he visited you?"

Strang said, "Yeah, he was falsely accusing the local chief of police of being in cahoots with the drugs guys." And he walked away.

Mickie watched him go. *Everyone knows the chief of police is in cahoots with the drug guys, and surely Strang would also know. So why does Strang accuse Holroyd of false accusations? I need to follow this up. Let me see if I can persuade the good professor to be more open.* She ran out of the building, but Holroyd was nowhere to be seen.

***

Holroyd returned to find Philip had been discharged from hospital. They went over to the cantina and ordered coffee. They sat and talked about getting run down by the cruise ship.

"I still don't understand why the ship didn't stop to see if there were survivors." Holroyd took a sip. "It goes against a basic marine law in a collision to investigate before going on."

"Perhaps no one realised there had been a collision."

"I suppose that is possible," Holroyd acknowledged. "But what will happen to the men who crewed our boat and their families?"

"I'll follow up to find out if the bodies were recovered and had a proper burial. As for the families, I don't know if they can get compensation from the cruise ship company, but I'll see what can be done." He hesitated as if a thought had struck him. "The trouble is, I suspect the company will fight any demand, and no one has the funds for a legal battle. I'm not very hopeful."

"Not very encouraging, I agree." Holroyd nodded and changed the subject to report on his meeting with Jimenez. After listening, Philip asked, "Who else knows of this meeting?"

"No one," Holroyd replied, "At least, no one I know of."

"I think we had better assume someone does," Philip observed. "Better to be safe than sorry." He got up, went to another room, and returned with a cell phone.

"People could track you by tracking and probably listening to your phone calls. Take this one and use it when you don't want anyone to know where you are or with whom you are talking," he said. "Keep using your old one so you don't get people excited by suddenly disappearing."

With that, they went to the cantina, where Mickie found them.

Chapter 21

Holroyd and Philip were enjoying a light meal when Mickie entered and went straight to their table.

"Professor Holroyd," she greeted them and, without invitation, sat down. She turned to Philip. "And may I know who you are?"

Before Philip could answer, Holroyd asked, "What is it you want now?"

"Why are you accusing the chief of police?"

"Accusing him?" asked Holroyd, surprised. "Who says so, and of what am I supposed to be accusing him?"

"Do you deny the allegation?"

"I don't accuse him of anything," Holroyd replied. "I have neither the reason nor the facts to do so. Now, if you have no further questions, please leave us to enjoy our lunch."

"So, you are telling me my information is incorrect," Mickie insisted.

"I have no idea what information you were given," Holroyd remarked, "or by whom. But from what you are asking me, I would say you have been misinformed."

"My information comes from an impeccable source, and … " Mickie started, but Philip broke in.

"Young lady," he said, "Professor Holroyd has given you his answer. Now, if you don't mind, he and I have business to discuss, so be so good as to take your leave."

Mickie looked at him and stood up. "Thank you, Professor." She turned to leave, but not before Holroyd thought he saw a triumphant gleam in her eyes.

"Who is she?" Philip asked, and Holroyd explained how she had made contact.

"I think you had better watch your back with that one," Philip observed.

Chapter 22

Merry went to his study and sat down behind his father's desk. Before he could do anything, the phone rang.

"Your Grace," Sir John opened the call , "I wonder if you would stop by at your earliest convenience. We should discuss your position."

"Indeed, we do," Merry replied, "In the light of my new responsibilities, I don't think I can continue in the Service. However, I would first like to finish my present assignment."

"I'm not sure that is appropriate," Sir John replied. "You are, after all, a member of the House of Lords and, as such, not eligible to continue in the Service."

"Sir John," Merry chided. "I have not yet been invested with the title, and I am not a member of the upper house until I am."

"This is most unusual, Your Grace," Sir John commented. "Is there any reason why I should support your request?"

"I believe so," Merry answered, "but not over the phone."

"I see," Sir John answered and, after a pause, went on. "I will defer a decision until then."

The phone rang, but Merry did not recognize the number and was about to refuse the call when he noticed the country of origin was Mexico. It was Holroyd.

Quickly, Holroyd reported he was using a new phone to evade listeners and went on to report what he had learned from Jimenez.

"So, this chief of police is somehow linked to the release of that cruise ship, but Jimenez thinks the order came from somewhere else."

"That's it in a nutshell."

"Thanks, Peter," Merry replied. "That's very helpful. Now tootle off to find your Chinese monument."

He thought about his next move and suddenly realised he had never questioned how Song had arrived at his door. He called the boy into his study.

"Now tell me about your background and how you arrived here." Song suddenly looked frightened.

"Why? Are you going to send me away?"

"No," answered Merry," I never asked you before and now I need to know how you ended up helping me out of my club that night. Start at the beginning."

"I grew up in a small village by the side of a river." Song seemed reassured. "Our house was small and built on stilts over the water. My father was a fisherman, my mother did the cooking and sewing, and I had two older brothers and a sister. When my father had an accident and couldn't fish anymore, we became very poor with little to eat. Then one day a man came to our home and offered to buy my sister, but when he saw me, he offered to buy us both. My mother accepted and I was taken to become a house boy in a rich man's house."

"What did you do there?"

"I was told that I had to work to repay the man who had bought me. So, I had to help clean the garage and the garden and go with another servant to the market to fetch vegetables. The man's wife was horrible and used to beat me with a stick and often sent me to bed without supper."

"Anything else?"

"Like what?"

"Provide favours… sexual favours."

"No."

"One afternoon, she beat me so hard I could not sleep, so I ran away. When I got into the city, I would beg for food, sometimes even steal from market stalls. I slept in alleyways and doorways, anywhere I could find shelter. That's when Siva found me and took me to the club. That was fun, being with other boys, getting fed and given pocket money to buy clothes, and I even sent money to my mother."

"Did you tell her what you were doing?"

"No."

"Did you like what you were doing?"

"Some of the clients were nice, but some were awful. When they had been drinking, they could be very rough."

"Why did you stay?"

"It was OK, and the manager told us that if we behaved well and stayed long enough, we would be given help to start a new career."

"And then what?"

Song explained how he had been blamed when a client died but was then given to this police lieutenant who delivered him to a Chinese man. That man arranged for him to be escorted to England, where he was told what he had to do.

"Were you promised anything?"

"Yes. My freedom and money."

"Do you remember the names of any of these people?"

"The police lieutenant's name was Thanaphon, and here, it was Mr. Cheng."

"Thank you," Merry replied, "now go and help mother."

When Song was out of the study, Merry called an acquaintance and asked that Mr. Cheng be found and held for questioning. He suggested calling his club's manager to get some details about where Cheng could be found.

He was about to call Wen Mei Li with what he had learned when he realised it would be late night in China, and instead reached for the midday editions of the newspapers that were on his desk.

On page three of the second paper he opened, he noted a headline 'English Professor wanted for murder.' He was about to ignore it when he caught sight of the name 'Holroyd.' Only then did he start reading the whole article.

Written by Jeanne-Michelle Desforestier, in Acapulco, he read 'The Chief of police, Jorge de Falta, today issued an arrest warrant in the name of Professor Peter Holroyd for the murder of Miguel Corredas, a waiter at Maria's cantina. Corredas was at work when he was brutally shot by two men later identified as having connections to Holroyd. Holroyd is suspected to be working with a drug cartel in Mexico.'

The rest of the article gave details of Holroyd's past problems elsewhere[10] and a suggestion that he was protected by highly placed individuals in England and China. It also mentioned Holroyd's son, Sean, had recently died in an Alpine accident.

"Stone the crows," Merry gasped. "What has Peter been up to?"

Phone calls to Peter and again Wen Mei Li went unanswered.

Next, he called the British Embassy in Bern and requested details of Sean. The reply confirmed the Alpine tragedy but that the *Obwalden Kantons Polizei* had not released the names pending confirmation of any victims and, if any, notification of the next of kin.

I'll wait until I get further information before I get back to Peter—no point in getting him worried until then.

---

[10] The Dragon's Threat and Gold among the Trees.

Chapter 23

Philip and Holroyd returned home and were settling down when there was a knock on the door. Philip answered it and came back accompanied by a man well-dressed in a business suit.

"Peter, this is Manuel, Private Secretary to Don Luis." The man bowed to Holroyd.

"Señor, Don Luis requests you and Brother Philip come with me to the Consulate now." Holroyd looked up in surprise and asked, "Why now?"

Manuel continued. "It is a matter of urgency."

"May I ask why?"

"Don Luis will explain at the Consulate, *Señor.*"

Holroyd looked at Philip and said, "I think we'd better go."

They were shown to a limousine with black tinted windows and drove off. On arrival at the consulate, they entered through a backdoor and went straight to Don Luis' study, where the consul awaited them.

"Welcome, gentlemen," Don Luis greeted them. "Please be seated, and Manuel will bring us coffee."

Holroyd was surprised that the task had been delegated to Manuel rather than to one of the staff but said nothing. Once Manuel arrived bringing the tray, Don Luis came to the point.

"Please accept my apologies for the manner of asking you to come over, but I believe circumstances suggest it was necessary." He looked at Holroyd. "I am convinced, Professor, you have become a target for assassination."

Holroyd's heart thumped and he grabbed the handkerchief in his pocket to wipe the sweat threatening to trickle down his temple.

"I knew it," commented Philip. "Peter, I warned you against talking in public."

"But I haven't," Holroyd managed to croak out.

"Then how did you get noticed?" asked Philip.

"I believe Professor Holroyd," interjected Don Luis. "But my information comes from sources that I trust."

"I agree it's pointless to talk about the source," Holroyd said, "I think the safest is that I disappear until matters cool down and I focus on my search for the stele."

"I agree," Don Luis said, "here is what I propose." He took a sip of coffee. "Even if you do not disappear, people must think you have disappeared. So we will arrange a deception. There is a ship in the harbour, La Estrella that leaves today for Panama and the East Coast of America. Professor Holroyd will go on board."

Don Luis looked to see if Holroyd had any objections, and when Holroyd said nothing, he continued." To do this, Manuel will drive one of my staff, dressed to look like the professor, to the ship where that man will embark. Manuel will use the professor's phone to make a call...it doesn't matter to whom, but then he will disable the phone. Manuel will return, and once the ship is out of the port, my man will disembark with the pilot." He motioned to Manuel to refill the coffee cups before continuing.

"Anyone watching or tracking the professor should be convinced he embarked and made a call before the ship sailed. If anyone asks the ship for confirmation, they will be told no Professor Holroyd is onboard, but that is the answer they would expect if they thought some agency employed Holroyd. A warm welcome will be waiting for the good professor in Panama."

There was silence. Then Manuel spoke, "Gentlemen, this is a scene we have practiced before. The drive to the ship will be in a car with black windows, so someone might only see the passenger when he goes up the gangway before disappearing below decks. That is a risk, but we think it's small and better than trying to hide the professor or smuggling him out of the country."

"And what do I do?" asked Holroyd.

"You go look for your Chinese monument," answered Don Luis. "We can help you on your way."

***

"Yes?" Strang looked up.

"Holroyd's gone dark," the operative reported, "Last ping was in the docks, and we have a report he was seen boarding a freighter that's left for Panama."

"Get me everything we have on that ship, including its final destination. And let me know if Holroyd surfaces anywhere."

The operative nodded and left. Strang sat for a moment and then picked up the phone.

Chapter 24

Holroyd and Philip were given peasant's clothes and seated in a covered truck driven towards the Guatemalan border. As far as Philip had determined, the possible site of the stele was near an archeological expedition exploring a recent find of ruins there. The truck was on its weekly run bringing supplies to the expedition.

The road was surprisingly good, and the driver informed them it had been built by a Chinese mining company excavating near their destination. Lulled by the smooth ride, Holroyd napped most of the way and was only jolted into full wakefulness when the truck branched off onto a track that had been hewed out of the jungle but led to the campsite.

Once they arrived and exited the truck, the heat and humidity struck with full force, and Holroyd was soon sweating.

He looked around. The camp had been set up in a clearing bordered on all sides by trees and undergrowth, but rectangular pyramidal shapes could be seen among the vegetation on two sides.

Tents had been set up, and a latrine had been dug near enough for convenience but far away so as not to be a danger by contamination.

People were busy in one tent Holroyd thought was the work tent, and another tent was the kitchen, given the cooking smells coming from there. Holroyd's stomach growled at the smell of vegetables and meat intermingling with freshly baked bread. A portable generator growled next to the kitchen, but as witnessed by nearby unopened boxes, more work remained.

The arrival of the truck was greeted with calls for people to come over to help unload.

"Oh! Who are you?" One of the helpers came over to Holroyd and Philip.

"How did you know we are English?" asked Holroyd, surprised.

"That's easy," the man laughed, "All that's missing is a Union Jack tattooed on your foreheads. I'm Fred Morrison, and I lead this motley crew. So, what brings you to this outpost of civilisation?"

"Peter Holroyd," Holroyd introduced himself. "And this is Brother Philip who wanted to come along for some excitement."

"Not sure how much excitement we can offer unless you're into Mexican archeology," remarked Morrison. By this time, other team members had gathered around, curious about the visitors.

"No," Holroyd answered, "Mexican archeology is outside my field. I'm looking into a report about a Chinese stele somewhere near here."

"Chinese stele?" Morrison asked doubtfully. "What's that?"

Holroyd asked for a piece of paper and a pencil and sketched what a stele looked like. Morrison looked at it and said, "I don't think there's anything like this around here."

One of his team asked to look at the drawing and said. "Wait a moment. I've seen something like this about a mile or two away. Young Juanito showed it to me." He turned to Holroyd. "Juanito is one of the children from the pueblo, about an hour's trek from here. Maybe I can get him to show you." Holroyd became very excited.

"Could you? That would be marvellous." At that moment, a loud boom reverberated across the site.

"Don't worry, "Morrison observed. "That's just explosives the Chinese use in their mining operation."

"Mining operation?"

"Yes, apparently there's a deposit of a rare mineral near here, and the Chinese have a licence to exploit it," Morrison explained. "We had a visit from them. They were curious about our activities but when it became clear there would be no overlap, they were quite cordial. However, they warned us there is a small group of bandits around here. Something tied to the drugs business, but what isn't in Mexico? Asked if we were armed, and I told them we have a rifle to scare off any animals, including predators, but that's it."

"Predators?" asked Holroyd nervously.

"Oh, mostly monkeys that get too curious but run if we make a big bang. They scarper into the bush," explained Morrison. "But jaguars are around, so we must take some precautions."

"And brigands," added another member of the group.

"Brigands?" asked Holroyd with a slight tremor in his voice.

Simultaneously, Philip asked, "Have you seen any?"

"Not so far," Morrison replied, "and I hope we never will. But we have to be ready in case we do." He stopped. "Now, both of you are welcome to stay as long as necessary. We'll find a place for you to sleep but you'll be sharing accommodation, and I will expect you to help around the camp. You can tell us more about yourselves this evening after dinner, but in the meantime, you are also welcome to look around the site."

He hesitated as if deciding what to. say next , and then said . "Just don't touch anything, but if you find something, let one of the team know. Who knows, you might even develop an interest in Mexican archeology.

Pottering around the site, Holroyd did not develop an interest in Mexican archeology, but he did wonder at the skills of the ancient builders. He also developed an awareness of the natural inhabitants of this area of the Mexican jungle but only sometimes enjoyed his new knowledge. He saw and heard various birds, some of which bore gloriously coloured plumage.

On the other hand, he was never sure which local insects were harmless and which carried a variety of unpleasant illnesses about which he had read. But none of this stopped him from becoming increasingly impatient so that the arrival of Juanito was most welcome.

Chapter 25

Juanito turned out to be a small child, perhaps ten or twelve years old, with a mix of central American and elfin features, but with a look of intelligence that suggested wisdom beyond his age. Once the mission was explained to him he nodded and beckoned Holroyd and Philip to follow him.

"Take water and insect protection with you," advised one team member. As they set out, the boom of another explosion from the Chinese mine reverberated across the camp.

Juanito set out at a brisk pace but slowed as he realised neither Holroyd nor Philip was used to walking through the jungle. They followed a scarcely recognisable track that Holroyd thought might be more of an animal track than a human path.

Juanito led the way, occasionally using a machete to hack away at foliage that impeded their progress.

Holroyd sweated in the heat and began to feel uncomfortable in his clammy shirt. However, that aside, the going was relatively easy, although Holroyd felt uneasy when he thought he once heard the cough of a jaguar and several times the slithering of reptiles but saw neither.

Soon, Holroyd began to feel tired and wondered how much further they had to go. As they continued,

Holroyd began to feel dizzy and even lost his footing several times. Philip watched him with mounting concern asking him how he felt and suggested a stop to rest and to eat and drink something. Holroyd refused, and they went on, albeit at a slower pace.

Finally, Juanito stopped in a small clearing and pointed at a mound covered in vegetation.

"*Aquí lo tienes,* "he said. "Here it is," Philip translated.

Holroyd looked doubtfully at the mound wondering how to clear the vegetation, but Philip turned to Juanito who nodded and began to slash at the growth. When a large batch of growth fell to the ground, parts of a stone object could be seen.

"Stop," Holroyd ordered and went up to the object. Clearing more vegetation with his hands, he saw a carved symbol.

Holroyd peered at it and tried to clear away some lichen that stubbornly refused to move but stopped realising he needed tools to complete the task. Nevertheless, he thought the symbol looked like ancient Chinese script and felt a surge of elation and excitement. *I think I've found it.* He stepped back, inviting Philip to have a look.

"I think this is it," he said, trying but failing to remain calm.

"Really? Well done," Philip looked carefully at the incision and gave Holroyd a congratulatory slap on the back. Suddenly, Philip jumped back as a large snake slithered from underneath the growth.

"That's a dangerous one," he said, "one bite can be fatal."

Philip turned to Juanito and said something at which the young man grinned and decapitated the reptile with a hefty swing. Holding the snake's body aloft, Juanito rubbed his tummy, suggesting it would make a good meal, but Philip shook his head. "I think we'd better be more careful; there could be more of those things around here."

"That's very encouraging," said Holroyd, "I hate snakes and insects." Holroyd gingerly approached the stonework, pausing every so often to make sure nothing was lying in wait to attack him and took out his cell phone and photographed the find. When he had finished, he turned to Philip.

"We've got to come back tomorrow to clear more of this stuff away," he motioned at the growth. "I'll ask Morrison for help, or at least some tools we'll need."

He reached into his pocket and took out a fold of cash. Peeling off the first bill he gave it to Juanito, who reacted with amazement and delight. "Ask Juanito if he will guide us again tomorrow," he said.

"I'd say that after the $100 you just gave him, Juanito will be very happy to do so," Philip remarked and then turned to Juanito, who nodded eagerly.

Once back at the camp, Holroyd reported what he had found to the team, all of whom were impressed. Morrison looked carefully at the photographs.

"I'd have to agree that these are promising indications you've found something worth further examination." He paused. "I won't spare anyone now, but I can let you have some tools. If you come back with better evidence, I'll see what we can do to help. It would be a major discovery if it is what you suspect it could be."

Chapter 26

Prepared for the day's excursion, Juanito again led the way. After about half an hour, Holroyd suddenly ordered, "Stop." He stood listening carefully, but Philip at first heard nothing unusual.

"Did you hear that?" Holroyd asked. He listened carefully and said, "that sounded like popping sounds, but what could make such sounds?"

Philip listened but heard nothing more.

Holroyd again heard the sounds. "What's that?" he asked. He listened again

"That's not usual; that sounded like gunfire to me," said Holroyd. "I think we should go back." He addressed Juanito, and after a moment, the boy nodded and pointed the way back. With that gesture, he scampered off in the direction they were originally going.

"Come on," said Holroyd.

"Why?" asked Philip.

"I think something's not right." And he set off back to the camp briskly, with Philip resignedly following. Knowing the route, they managed a fast pace, and the return trek took only 20 minutes. Approaching the camp, they heard a shot followed by yells and more shots.

Controlling their first instincts to rush into camp, they hesitated before creeping forward softly. Near the edge of the camp, they found some dense foliage in which they could hide and see what was happening.

They saw a group of men, several brandishing weapons, standing around the team members who had been herded into a small group.

Holroyd saw Professor Morrison talking animatedly with one of the attackers while the rest of the team cowered under the menacing watch of their guards.

Suddenly, there was a shot, and Morrison fell to the ground. He did not move, and Holroyd realised Morrison had just been murdered in cold blood. The bandit looked at the body and spat on it. Turning to his men, he gave an order, and within a minute or so, the entire team was massacred.

Holroyd almost vomited but managed to control himself. He watched the attackers leisurely going through the camp, collecting anything of value. He felt a wave of disgust as one of the attackers ripped the underwear off one of the dead girls and gleefully sniffed them to the boisterous amusement of his comrades.

The leader gave an order and two of the men dragged the bodies into a heap and made a half-hearted effort to cover the grisly mound.

Shaken by what he witnessed; Holroyd suddenly noticed two men chatting with the bandit leader. With shock, he recognised Li Feng and Strang.

He had first met Li Feng in Canada when Li Feng's employer wanted to engage Holroyd to help recover lost treasure.[11] At that time, Li Feng looked his part as the suave, successful Hong Kong consultant, but he had disappeared after the death of his employer.

The intervening years had not been kind, because Li Feng had lost weight, and his skin was not as healthy as it had been. In addition, his face was etched with lines that gave it a cruel and feral look.

Holroyd suddenly shivered at the thought he might meet Li Feng face to face again. *If we do, Li Feng will want to have his revenge. I've got to make sure that doesn't ever happen.*

He felt a trickle of sweat run down his back and had an urge to urinate. Reaching out, Holroyd grasped Philip's arm. "I know two of those two men," he whispered. "The taller one is Li Feng, someone I had the misfortune to meet several years ago, but what is he doing here? The other is Strang, the American poohbah here."

---

[11] Gold among the trees

"I didn't recognise him, but you're right," Philip whispered back. "But why do those bandits know him?"

Just then, three men came out of the jungle, two armed. One of the bandits opened fire, and one of the armed men fell. The other two dropped into a prone position, and the armed man started shooting back with an automatic rifle. Three bandits dropped dead or wounded while the others started firing back.

"Stop," yelled Li Feng in Spanish and then in English. His yell carried enough weight that the firing stopped.

"Come out of there with your hands up," commanded Li Feng in Spanish and then English.

The unarmed man slowly rose with his arms in the air while his companion remained in a firing position. With his arms still in the air, the man approached Li Feng and Holroyd saw he was Chinese.

Li Feng, recognising a countryman, opened the conversation in Chinese, and after a short dialogue, turned to the man whom neither Holroyd nor Philip could identify.

"This man is a foreman at the mine," he explained. "He was sent to find out what the gunfire was about."

"Tell him it's of no concern of his," answered the man. Li Feng turned back to the foreman, and they spoke again. The foreman wasn't happy to get that reply. Li Feng turned back to the man.

"He said he could ignore the whole incident," Li Feng reported, "however one of his men has been killed, and he will have to report that."

"Tell him to report an animal attacked the man," was the reply.

"That would be a reasonable report if someone can explain which animal uses bullets to attack humans," observed Li Feng drily.

He turned back to the foreman, who was now talking animatedly on his cell phone. The man said, "Stop him," and lunged forward to grab the phone when a spurt of dirt at his feet erupted from a shot from the prone man.

"I rather think we're too late," observed Li Feng. "We had better leave before the whole Chinese army arrives." He turned back to the foreman, who nodded and watched as the bandits and their loot disappeared into the jungle.

Satisfied peace had returned, and it was as safe as could be, the prone man stood up but dropped again as Holroyd and Philip came out of the bush with hands in the air.

The foreman beckoned the pair while saying something to the gunman, who remained in the firing position.

"*Ni hao. Women shi pengyoumen*," Holroyd yelled.

"What are you saying?" hissed Philip.

"I'm telling them we are friends," answered Holroyd.

"*Ni hui shuo Zhong wen!*" the foreman replied, surprised, and then switched to English. "Be so kind as to explain who you are and why you are here." The gunman remained in his position covering the pair.

"Excuse me for a moment." Holroyd gasped and moved to the edge of the clearing to relieve himself. Now composed again, Holroyd explained who they were and why they were here.

"And what has all this to do with you?" the foreman waved his arm towards the carnage.

After Holroyd reviewed the morning's events, the foreman said, "You obviously cannot stay here. Come with us, and we will arrange for your return once we are at our camp." And with that, the gunman hoisted his dead companion on his shoulders, and the foreman picked up the dead man's weapon.

The four set off to where a jeep was parked behind some tree; the foreman spoke briefly to his companion, who nodded and returned to the camp.

"He will collect our spent cartridges," the foreman explained. "We don't need to let anyone know we were involved in a gunfight." While they waited, the foreman talked with someone back at their camp.

Once the call was over, the foreman engaged Holroyd in conversation wondering how Holroyd came to speak Chinese. Finally, the rifleman returned with the spent cartridges, and the group returned to their camp.

Once arrived, Holroyd and Philip met with the mine manager who looked at Holroyd and Philip before engaging in a lively conversation with the foreman.

"Well, gentlemen," the manager turned to Holroyd and Philip. "I am Wang Su, the mine manager here and I have just been informed of the tragedy at the archeological site. I am happy that you survived that terrible experience."

"Wang Su," Holroyd replied. "I am Peter Holroyd, and this is my friend Philip Smythe-Jones. Please accept our gratitude for your assistance."

"Please do not mention it," Wang Su answered. "We could do no less. In any case, you are welcome to recover from your troubles, although our hospitality cannot meet the standards you are doubtlessly accustomed to."

"Your hospitality doubtlessly exceeds any standards we might have," said Holroyd, and Wang Su nodded appreciating the observation of Chinese etiquette.

"Please refresh yourselves and when it is convenient, perhaps you can explain how all this happened."

They were led to a hut where they could bathe before getting a meal and rest. Holroyd used the time to call Merry and give him a full report, including the presence of Li Feng and Strang.

"Who is Strang?" asked Merry.

"Supposedly the local representative of the DEA, but I think he's much more. I think he's involved with Li Feng and the local cartels."

"From what you've just told me, I agree," observed Merry, "and that's just one more line of inquiry."

He stopped and asked, "What did you learn about the gang attacking the camp?"

"Nothing," replied Holroyd and hung up.

They were summoned back to Wang Su's office.

"I trust you are well rested, gentlemen," Wang Su observed. "Perhaps you can tell me what happened. Holroyd gave a full report.

"Thank you," Wang Su said, "I have informed my headquarters of the event and have been told to look after you for the time being. However, the occurrence raises some interesting questions about the activity of these bandits and the safety of our enterprise." He then added. "We shall have to prepare in case unannounced visitors should knock on our doors."

***

Wen Mei Li went through the reports on her desk and one item caught her attention. The cruise ship Distant Horizon had arrived in its home port. *Isn't that the ship that was held in Acapulco because there were drugs on board? Why has it been allowed to continue? Maybe Peter has some contacts and can get some information.* She picked up the phone and Holroyd answered. She explained what she wanted, and Holroyd reported what he had been told.

Wen Mei Li sat back and thought *I know of one Chinaman in Vietnam who could order such a transport of drugs, Li Feng! Could this be him? If so, we've finally got a solid lead. I wonder where he is right now.* She picked up the phone and started calling around.

Next, she called Merry on their private line. The discussion was short and to the point.

"We've got a possible suspect to follow up. His name is Li Feng."

"Li Feng?" asked Merry, surprised.

147

"You sound surprised," Wen Mei Li observed.

"Yes, I am," answered Merry. "The vice squad in Bangkok started cleaning house and caught one of its lieutenants in the net. Hang on, let me get the name for you." He stopped. "Ah! Yes, a Lieutenant Thanaphon. Apparently, he was prominent in procuring boys for the sex trade in America and Europe. But he reported to none other than to a Li Feng."

"How very convenient!" Wen Mei Li observed. "Matters are developing at a most satisfactory pace." She switched to another topic. "Have you read about the attack on our mining camp in Mexico, near where that archeological team was just massacred?"

"Yes, but I didn't give much attention," Merry replied. "I didn't think it was connected to anything I'm looking at."

"Li Feng is in Mexico, and I can guess why," she commented after getting Merry's report. "Perhaps it's time we did a bit of cleaning in that area of Mexico. The Chinese people do not take it lightly when bandits start killing one of their citizens. And I have just been told Holroyd has been taken under the protection of the Chinese Mining company. The problem is getting him away without alerting Li Feng or anyone else targeting him."

"I asked our people to help, and their reply was less than helpful," Merry reported. "In essence, I was told His Majesty's Government is not about to ask the Mexican government to help retrieve a British national who is reported to be involved in the illegal drugs business."

"How did they come to that conclusion?" asked Wen Mei Li.

"Seems they read that article by that Canadian journalist," commented Merry.

"But that is garbage," protested Wen Mei Li.

"We both know that," answered Merry, "but the stuffed heads over in Whitehall prefer to believe it." He remarked. "I think they're just shying away from getting involved."

"My government got a very uncooperative response from the Mexicans," Wen Mei Li reported. "We asked for protection of our people at the mine and offered to supply troops if Mexico could not. The Mexicans told our people to stay out of it as Mexico could handle its own affairs. Any armed arrivals from China without the prior approval of the Mexican government would be considered an act of war. When we asked when protection would be available, we were told that Mexico has its priorities and will handle this as soon as possible."

"So, what next?" asked Merry.

"There is no prohibition for the mine to receive additional mining personnel," replied Wen Mei Li somewhat smugly. "I believe they are already on their way." She paused. "I am told they have had other training to improve their mining techniques."

Merry hung up and decided he should contact the NCA to set up a meeting. Next, he looked for any message from the Embassy in Bern and was told everyone was accounted for. Sean Holroyd was safe.

"That's a relief," Merry muttered, "at least I won't be the bearer of bad news."

Chapter 27

Holroyd and Philip left the canteen and returned to their quarters. They were climbing the external stairs and missed the arrival of the jeep at the mine's front gate.

Two men got out and were soon in discussion with one of the hands when one of the men grasped the arm of the other and pointed to Holroyd and Philip, who were entering their dormitory. The hand looked up, and the three men conversed further before the visitors drove off.

"Gentlemen," Wang Su summoned Holroyd and Philip and reported the visit. "Qu Wang informs me two men, a white man, and a Chinaman, arrived here a short while ago. They saw you and asked who you two were." He stopped. "Qu Wang said you were visitors, and the two men left. However, I believe these were the same two men you saw at the massacre of the archeological team."

"Damn!" Holroyd shifted nervously. "That being so, they are a danger to you and us, and I do not feel comfortable staying here. Can you arrange transport for us to leave?"

"I agree," Wang Su replied, "I will arrange for you to leave immediately with the convoy of trucks that will be delivering our next consignment of ore to the port."

Holroyd looked at Philip and then back to Wang Su. "I think that's best," he said. "Thank you for your help and hospitality."

"Thank you for your cooperation," Wang Su replied. "Each cab has a space behind the driver where he normally keeps some tools and supplies. It's a tight fit, but I suggest you hide there for the first half hour. You can sit with the driver once you are away from here. Now please hurry as the trucks will leave in a few minutes."

Holroyd got into the first truck and after much showing and pushing accompanied by what Holroyd took to be ribald jokes at his expense, found himself wedged into the space behind the driver. There was a curtain between him and the driver, but he had drawn it partially so that he could see forward.

The truck moved forward with a grinding of gears but eventually smoothed out to maintain a steady pace. The road was narrow with a ditch and jungle at the edges, but the driver seemed familiar and drove at a pace Holroyd found alarming. Nevertheless, Holroyd was not unduly worried and looked forward to when he could safely come out from his hiding place.

They rounded a curve and came face to face with four vehicles coming in the opposite direction. Holroyd noted that each vehicle carried men armed with rifles or machine guns. He began to sweat and noticed his hand was trembling. *These men are probably after me. Thank goodness we left when we did.*

He had no further time to think as his driver and the driver of the lead vehicle tried to avoid an accident, but the truck was too heavy to stop quickly and hit the lead vehicle with sufficient force that the vehicle overturned into the ditch. All the other vehicles and the trucks came to a stop.

For a few moments, all that could be heard was the growl of the truck engines, but then men brandishing their weapons ran to surround the trucks, yelling as they did so.

Gesturing the drivers to get out of the trucks, men clambered up to see inside the driver's cabs. But the drivers sat immobile, which infuriated the attackers even more. At that moment, a face appeared at the cab door of Holroyd's truck, and one of the attackers looked carefully over the interior.

Holroyd froze and held his breath, as the man continued to look carefully even trying to peer under the dashboard. To Holroyd, it seemed like an eternity before the attacker stepped away from the cab and Holroyd heard him say "*Nada aqui.*" Holroyd's driver turned to face Holroyd and smiled.

Holroyd ventured to stick his head out of his hiding place and get a better view. He saw the overturned vehicle and more men rushing to the trucks. Just as matters appeared to turn ugly, Holroyd saw two men clamber out of the overturned vehicle.

One was Li Feng, who appeared to be bleeding from a gash on his head, while the other was the driver, who needed assistance to stand and was holding his left arm as if it was broken or the shoulder dislocated.

Holroyd heard Li Feng talking to someone in Chinese and guessed it was with the man in charge of the truck convoy. Holroyd dared not to move and resigned himself to wait more for the moment he could get out of his cramped quarters. Finally, the conversation ended, and Li Feng turned to one of the attackers, who shrugged his shoulders and gave an order to his men.

Several went over to put the lead vehicle back on the road; others went back to their vehicles and began to reverse their vehicles and allow the trucks to move on, while the remainder stood by the wayside, watching the trucks resume their journey.

Above the sound of the truck's growling engine, Holroyd did not hear the sound of gunfire back at the camp.

***

The ore trucks stopped at a warehouse on the city's outskirts, and Holroyd and Philip were told to get out. Once out, the trucks continued on their way, leaving the two men standing in a dusty paved courtyard with no one in sight.

Both men started sweating in the heat, gratefully stretching their limbs, and decided to see if they could get a lift when Manuel arrived in the consul's limousine.

"Gentlemen, please get in out of the heat," Manuel invited them, holding the back door open. Once in, Manuel drove off.

"The consul has decided that it is not safe for either of you in Acapulco but has arranged for you to fly out. We are heading for the airport where you will collect your tickets to England and depart immediately for Mexico City, where you will change planes."

"That is extremely generous of the consul," said Holroyd, "but I must decline. I won't leave before satisfying myself about the stele."

"*Señor*," Manuel protested, "the consul feels strongly you are not safe in Acapulco, and he may not be able to help you again."

"I understand, Manuel," Holroyd said, "but my mind is made up."

"*Señor,* you could come back when conditions are safer," Manuel continued his protest, "but it would be best for you to leave now."

"Sorry, Manuel," Holroyd said.

"Can you not persuade the professor?" Manuel turned to Philip.

"I agree with you, Manuel," replied Philip, "but I don't think. I can persuade him."

"And yourself, *señor*?" Manuel asked Philip.

"Thank the consul, but I'm also not leaving. My parishioners need me, and I have already been way too long."

"Philip," Holroyd said, "I really don't think that's a good idea. You won't be any good to your flock if you are incapacitated or even dead."

"Yes, I know that," Philip replied, "but I'm not changing my mind. Manuel, please drop me off when we get to a convenient place from where I can get home."

"Señor," Manuel replied, "I strongly suggest you not to do that. There is a limit to how far we can help you."

"I understand, and thank you," Philip answered, "but please follow my wishes." Manuel just shrugged his shoulders.

"I'll get out with you," Holroyd said.

"Thanks, old boy," Philip smiled. He and Holroyd out at an intersection and waved as the car returned to the consulate.

Holroyd and Philip decided that a meal would be in order and, believing they would be safe, went to a nearby restaurant. Philip entered the restaurant, but before Holroyd could do so, he was gripped from behind and dragged into a van that had just pulled up behind them. Philip turned at the commotion and saw Holroyd being bundled into a van that sped off.

The attack was so sudden and unexpected that Holroyd was unable to react before he was unceremoniously thrown to the van floor, and the door was slammed shut.

"What the hell is this?" Holroyd yelled but only got a painful kick in the ribs. Before he could utter another sound, his mouth was taped shut, a hood placed over his head and his wrists tied behind him. Another kick met a further grunt, and Holroyd lapsed into silence for the rest of the trip.

***

Wen Mei Li called Merry, "Did you know Holroyd was at the mine?"

"No!" exclaimed Merry. "Is he safe?"

"We don't know," answered Wen Mei Li. "We know he was safely taken back to town, and I am told he was given tickets to fly back to London, but he never boarded his plane. At this time, we are asking around."

"My goodness," Merry answered. "I have someone in Acapulco I can ask to help us."

"That would be most helpful," Wen Mei Li observed. "Thank you for your cooperation, your Grace."

"Hang on," Merry laughed embarrassedly. "I'm not there yet. But I'll get back to you as soon as I have anything to tell you." And with that, the call ended.

Merry picked up the phone and dialled a number that connected him to Jimenez in Mexico.

Chapter 28

"Your club just called," his secretary announced, "and would be grateful if you could stop by after work."

"Did they mention why?" Merry asked.

"No, Sir."

After work, Merry went to his club and waited at the bar, ordering a drink when the club duty manager approached him.

"Your Grace, it is a pleasure to welcome you again," he said obsequiously. "There is a gentleman who would like to speak with you."

"Is he a club member?" asked Merry. "Because if he is, he hardly needs your help to approach me."

"He is the guest of a member," the manager replied, but just then, a man pushed his way to stand next to Merry.

"Hello, old boy," the man greeted Merry but the tone hardly suggested friendliness.

"Am I supposed to know you?" asked Merry.

"Not at all," the man replied, "but we do have a common acquaintance who asked me to remind you to tread very carefully if you want to avoid any accidents that could happen to that catamite of yours." The man patted Merry on the arm and disappeared.

"Who sponsored that man?" Merry furiously turned on the manager.

"I received a phone request from a highly respected member that the man be admitted, but the sponsor might be delayed." The duty manager shifted nervously.

"How long have you been on staff here?" demanded Merry.

"Six months, your Grace," the manager replied miserably.

"That's long enough for you to have learned that guests are asked to wait in the lobby until the sponsor is present," Merry pointed out, still furious. "I will bring the matter to the attention of the club committee, who, I think, will consider this seriously. Now get out of my sight. Better yet, get out of the club."

Merry sipped his drink. *I have been warned again and must choose between Song and the Service.*

Chapter 29

Mickie decided to go to a nearby café and relax, but on the way, she bought an English newspaper. Sitting on the terrace and after ordering a cafecito, she started to read. Under glaring headlines, she read of the massacre of the archeological team by bandits, presumed to be part of a drug cartel. She noted that the team had American and Mexican members, although names were not given.

Sitting back, she wondered if it was another case of drug cartel violence or if there was anything different this time. With nothing else planned, she decided to see if Strang had anything useful.

So was excited by the article she left before noticing the article reporting an attack by bandits on the Chinese mining camp. Two bandits were wounded and possibly killed, and two mining engineers had received non-life-threatening gunshot wounds. The attackers were presumed to be related to one of the cartels.

On arrival at Strang's office, she noted an unusual activity and wondered why. Just then, Strang came out of his office and frowned when he caught sight of Mickie.

"What the hell do you want here?" he barked at her.

"I came to find out if you had anything new on the massacre of the archeological team."

"Why should I?" Strang answered brusquely. "It's probably just another example of cartel crime."

"Yes," answered Mickie, "but Americans were killed."

"Yes, they were," admitted Strang, "but that's the Department of State's problem, not mine."

"Then what is your problem?" asked Mickie innocently.

"For one, what was your Holroyd doing there, and why wasn't his body found?"

"Holroyd? How do you know that?" Mickie was surprised. *Did he expect Holroyd to be there and get killed?*

"We found Morrison's logbook," Strang answered. "He was the team leader and recorded daily events, including the arrival and stay of Holroyd and that friar friend of his. Morrison was killed before he entered that day's events, so we don't know what they did that day. What we do know is neither of them was found among the dead."

"Are you suggesting Holroyd was not killed?" Mickie asked.

"Looks like it," admitted Strang. "Because his body wasn't found, he was either kidnapped by the bandits or was somehow involved with them."

"Perhaps he hid, and the bandits didn't know he was there," Mickie said, "and once the coast was clear, he somehow got away."

"If that's so," Strang said, "Why hasn't he turned up, or why has no one heard from him?"

"But why would the bandits kidnap Holroyd?" wondered Mickie. "How would they know enough to want him, unless they thought he was worth ransoming."

"You got it, lady," answered Strang, "and that leaves him involved in the attack as the most likely explanation. And that tells me Holroyd is up to his scrawny neck in the drugs game."

"Oh! Wow," Mickie exclaimed. "That proves my suspicions."

"Yep," said Strang, "but don't even think of going public until you have cleared it with me. Is that clear?"

"If you insist," Mickie answered meekly.

"I do," Strang said.

Mickie left the building and decided to see if she could get some information from Philip, only to learn

he, too, was away and not expected back for a few
more days.

Chapter 30

Holroyd was brusquely taken from the van, searched, and, after his restraints had been removed, locked in a dark room. A few minutes later, a bucket, some tissues and a couple of water bottles were handed into the room, and Holroyd was left shivering and afraid to ponder his position.

Sitting in the dark, on the floor, Holroyd shivered and clasped his arms around his knees. *What now? I've done nothing to get to this point. Why have I been taken? And why? What about my family?* He stopped as a sob escaped. *"Are they going to kill me? I don't deserve to die, and who of my friends knows I'm here?* He felt tears running down his cheeks, and a small moan escaped from his lips.

The door opened, and a man stood silhouetted against the glare from outside

"Doctor Holroyd, we meet again," Li Feng announced.

"You, again?" Holroyd croaked. "I thought I had seen the last of you after our last meeting."

"I thought so too," Li Feng answered agreeably, "until I was informed of your presence here. Just why are you in Mexico?"

"I might ask you the same question," Holroyd replied, "I would hardly have expected to see you here, as I can't imagine there's Chinese treasure here." He stopped before going on, "At least, I thought that way until I saw you at the murder scene."

It suddenly dawned on him it might not be wise to be adversarial at this point, but outrage overcame caution, and he discarded the idea.

"You were at the archeological camp and saw the massacre?" Li feng exclaimed. "That, as you can readily realise, presents me with a problem. How can I let you go free to tell everyone what you witnessed?"

He looked at Holroyd. "But I am curious. As far as I know, you are not interested in ancient Mexican history, so why were you there?"

"That's none of your business," retorted Holroyd, trying to show he was not intimidated by Li Feng's presence.

"I seem to remember a similar response from you many years ago," Li Feng observed. "However, the circumstances are different, so you will agree that it is very much my business."

"If you think I have anything to say to you, you're very wrong." Holroyd maintained his show of bravado.

"I think you will come to find that you are very wrong," Li Feng said. "But we have time for you to answer my question." He stopped and took out what proved to be Holroyd's cell phone.

"In the meanwhile, there is another matter in which I am interested." He looked at Holroyd. "As I know you are." He showed Holroyd the photographs of the stele.

"Do you know what this symbol is?"

"Even if I do, I wouldn't tell you," Holroyd retorted defiantly.

"Then let me tell you what I know," Li Feng examined the photograph. "This is definitely Chinese. It's carved in a script in common use during the Ming Dynasty."

"Are you telling me this is evidence Zhou Man came here?" Holroyd sat up excited, his fears momentarily set aside.

"No," Li Feng answered. "There is not enough on this picture to show that."

"Then, what?"

"You probably don't know the full story of Zhou Man's voyage," Li Feng ignored Holroyd's question. "In fact, I don't think anyone does." He paused. "But I do know more than most people."

"Give me an example," Holroyd asked excitedly.

"He was carrying a lot of treasure," Li Feng replied," the whereabouts of which are unknown."

"And how do you know this?"

"I did a lot of research when I took on the late departed Wang's enterprise. At the time, I did not see any relevance for that task, but now I do for the task at hand." He waited to let Holroyd consider what had just been said.

"I have access to documents that few people know about." Li Feng grinned.

"And why are you telling me all this now?" asked Holroyd.

"I am thinking we could cooperate on finding out who these Chinese visitors were," Li Feng nodded at the photographs, "and see if they left anything here that would be worth recovering."

"And for whom would we recover whatever is there?" Holroyd retorted in a tone that conveyed he doubted there would be any benefit to himself.

"Come, come," Li Feng chided. "Did I not say we would cooperate? I am confident we will both benefit."

"Attractive as that offer is," Holroyd snorted. "I wouldn't cooperate with a murdering swine such as you, and anyway, I'm hardly in a position to cooperate even if I wanted to."

"Your opinion of me is of no consequence at this point, and if you decide to cooperate, your current situation can easily be improved."

"And if I decide not to cooperate?"

"That would be most regrettable, as I am sure you already realise," Li Feng told him before leaving Holroyd in the dark again.

Holroyd tried to control his fear and let his rational side kick in. *I've got to start thinking about what options are open to me. I can refuse to cooperate and risk that these people are bluffing about killing me, or I can cooperate with Li Feng and wait for an opportunity to escape. But can I trust Li Feng?*

He stopped to consider the question and went over his past experiences when he and Li Feng were hunting for Koxinga's treasure. *He wasn't as ruthless then as he seems to be now, but I believe he is realistic enough that he won't do anything drastic as long as he thinks he will get what he wants. That suggests cooperation is my best bet at this point.*

But then another thought hit him. *Who is behind my kidnapping? Are the bandits part of a cartel? Then the massacre would make sense if they thought the archeology team posed a threat. Then, if the bandits knew I had witnessed the massacre, they would've killed or snatched me to stop me from being a witness.* He stopped.

But If it's Li Feng who is behind this, why would he kidnap me? He only now found out about the stele. So he wants my help, and if he can stop the cartel from doing anything, then he must be in a position of authority with them and so very much involved with the distribution of drugs.

The only way I can follow through with all these thoughts will be if I survive long enough to do so, and at the moment, the only way open to me to survive seems to be to cooperate. That settles it. I'll agree to cooperate, for a while at least.

Chapter 31

Although Mickie failed to notice the report of the attack on the mining camp, Wen Mei Li did not. She picked up the phone, and after discussion, a dozen militarily trained mining engineers would be sent to Mexico to act as guards. At the same time, the Foreign Ministry would express China's alarm over the attacks and demand protection of the camp by Mexican Forces.

Chapter 32

Jimenez read the report of the abduction at the restaurant and called for CCTV recordings. When they arrived, he looked at them closely. He saw two men approaching the restaurant, but their backs were towards the camera, thus preventing recognition of the individuals.

One man had just entered but as the second was about to enter, a white van pulled up. Two men jumped out and grabbed the person and bundled him into the van, which then drove off. There were no identifying marks on the van's side, and the camera angle did not permit a full view of the license plate.

"More cartel thuggery," grumbled Jimenez, "and no information until someone comes forward to report a missing person…if they do. Just one more crime that won't get solved." He turned to the next report when his phone rang, and he answered.

"Good afternoon, sir," Merry's voice floated down the line. "I have a problem, and I hope you can help me."

"*Si señor,* "Jimenez answered in Spanish in case anyone was nearby to hear the conversation "*¿Le puedo ayudar en algo?*"

"A good friend, Peter Holroyd, is missing, and I would appreciate your assistance in finding him," Merry reported.

"Peter Holroyd? You say he is missing?"

Jimenez switched to heavily accented English again to benefit anyone listening in. "Let me get some details, and I can ask if anyone has information." Merry gave enough to satisfy any eavesdropper that this was a legitimate missing persons report. If there were questions as to why Jimenez had received the call, the explanation would include that the number had been used by mistake.

"Thank you, señor, "Jimenez ended the call with a "Leave a number with me, and someone will get back to you." He returned to his reading of events as one of his men stuck his head in the door and said "Teniente, that priest, Brother Philip, just reported his friend has been kidnapped outside a restaurant." Jimenez sat up. *That CCTV film is of Holroyd getting taken.*

Jimenez got up, informed the staff he was going for his lunch break, and left the office. Once outside the office, he used his cell phone to call Merry.

"You asked about Holroyd." Jimenez opened the conversation. "Is there anything you can tell me?"

Merry reported that Holroyd was supposed to have boarded planes to England but never arrived.

"When did this become apparent?"

"Yesterday," answered Merry.

"Then I have to tell you I think he was kidnapped as he was about to enter a restaurant here in Acapulco," Jimenez reported what he knew.

"Not again," exclaimed Merry, "that man attracts kidnappers like honey attracts wasps. I don't suppose you have any clue as to who was behind it this time."

Jimenez explained the van was not identified.

"Do you have any ideas?"

"Other than one of the cartels, no." Jimenez sounded resigned.

"What do you know about the American, Strang?" asked Merry.

"Only that he is supposed to be the DEA representative here. Why?"

"Just something that crossed my desk," Merry replied, "but I'm not sure it's relevant."

"I know that Strang and the *Jefe* get on well, but that's all." Jimenez said." Thank you, my friend, I will stay in touch." And the conversation ended. *But now I have work to do finding Holroyd as if I need that on top of the other problems I'm facing.*

Chapter 33

Holroyd blinked at the light when Li Feng opened the door.

"Well, Doctor," Li Feng said, "have you considered my offer?"

"Yes, I have," answered Holroyd, "but what conditions are there?"

"Only that you go to the site with a couple of my men and examine the object, take photographs, and report back to me."

"And after that?" asked Holroyd. "Your previous offers to me always contained conditions that I only learned about later."

"Come, come," Li Feng replied, "there are no further conditions, but there are also no promises as to what happens after you report back to me. I would say that your cooperation will serve both our purposes."

Holroyd considered what he had been told and then said, "I shall require a bath and good food, supplies for the excursion, and of course, the assistance of the boy Juanito, to get to the site." *I hope that they won't harm the boy.*

"Of course, I appreciate your cooperation." Li Feng stood aside and invited Holroyd to step outside.

Once out, Holroyd was escorted to an adjoining house, given a bath, fresh clothes, and a meal while two men were sent to fetch Juanito.

The men returned with Juanito, led by a rope halter around his neck. Holroyd was horrified by the rope and to see the boy's tear-stained and bloody face. Furiously, he turned to Li Feng.

"What are you doing? That's barbaric! How dare you treat the boy like that?"

"It appears he did not come willingly," Li Feng answered in an amused tone but also gave the order to remove the halter. Juanito stood there trembling and started to cry again.

Holroyd moved over to the boy and hugged him closely while stroking his head. "You'll be safe with me," he whispered in as comforting a tone as he could, though recognising the boy spoke no English. After a while, Juanito calmed down and put his arms around Holroyd. Holroyd faced Li Feng.

"If you want any cooperation from me, you will make damn sure the boy is not mistreated again."

"As you wish," Li Feng replied and said something to the men, who grinned but nodded. Li Feng turned back to Holroyd.

"What tools will you need?"

"A machete to remove vegetation, trowels and brushes to scrape away lichen, and a magnifying glass to see what I'm looking at, and of course photographic equipment."

"A cell phone will suffice for photography, and I'll see what is available for tools, but neither you nor the boy will be given weapons. One of the men will carry and use a machete." He stopped when Holroyd appeared to want to argue. "That is final."

Holroyd nodded.

"You and the boy will carry your equipment and supplies. The men will, of course, be armed with guns to make sure you don't try to run away."

"Of course, I expected no less," Holroyd answered resignedly.

"You leave tomorrow first light," Li Feng ordered, and the meeting ended.

Chapter 34

Mickie knocked on Philip's door and was informed he was at the cantina. She found him sitting alone at a table with a beer in front of him but carefully watching clients as they entered and sat down. He frowned as he caught sight of her.

Ignoring his displeasure, Mickie sat down. Philip looked at her in silence.

"I finally succeeded in finding you," Mickie opened the conversation.

"An event I would have gladly postponed indefinitely," retorted Philip icily.

"Anyway, I want you to confirm something for me." Mickie ignored Philip's manner.

"Really? I am surprised," Philip said. "I didn't think you wanted to confirm anything you're following."

"Look," Mickie replied defensively as if realising she was facing a high level of lack of cooperation. She adopted as conciliary a tone as she was able. "I think your friend Holroyd is in deep trouble, and I'd like to help him."

"Really?" asked Philip in a disbelieving tone. "Why?"

"I think he's in danger," Mickie said, "and I don't think it's his fault that he's in that position."

"I see," answered Philip, "and just how do you think you can help him?"

"By getting the facts and going public," answered Mickie, "that's what we do as journalists."

"I see," said Philip, "and what confirmation from me are you looking for?"

"Were you and he at the archeological camp when those archeologists were murdered?"

"No," answered Philip. *And please, God, don't hold this against me at the Pearly Gates.*

"Then where were you?"

"As I said, not at the camp," Philip replied.

"Did you or he witness the murders?"

"I have no idea what Peter may or may not have seen," replied Philip, "and as I said, I was not at the camp."

"I have a witness that says you were both at the camp," Mickie challenged Philip.

"Then, why are you looking for confirmation from me?"

"To verify the credibility of my witness," Mickie explained in a tone that might have been used to calm a fractious child

"I see," Philip acknowledged, "but I can't help you."

"A final question," Mickie changed tack. "Is Holroyd alive?"

"Oh my! I sincerely hope so." Philip sat up. "Do you have any reason to suspect he isn't?"

"No," Mickie stood up. "If he was at the camp, I'd have expected he would have been murdered too. But his body wasn't among the dead. And I find that strange."

"I wouldn't find it strange at all," Philip observed, "if he wasn't at the camp at that time."

"So where is your friend?"

"I have no idea," Philip answered, "and before you ask, I don't know who might."

"Are you telling me he has disappeared?"

"No," answered Philip, "I'm telling you; I don't know where he is right now."

"So...."Mickie was about to continue.

"Would you mind leaving now?" Philip interrupted her. "You interrupted my enjoyment of this excellent beer, and I'd rather like to get back to it."

Mickie looked at him, surprised by his interruption, but finally nodded and walked out.

Philip watched her leave with a sense of relief. *I do not trust her at all. She is far too nosy about Peter, and I am not telling her he's been kidnapped. God knows what she'd do if she knew that.*

He drained his glass and ordered a refill and a burrito. *But that's the problem with these young, eager beaver journalists: no idea of manners! Not a word of apology for the interruption or a word of thanks for my cooperation.*

Chapter 35

Juanito stayed close to Holroyd as they set out. The two guards followed with rifles slung and machetes and pistols in their belts. *They look like extras in some cheap Mexican bandit movie,* thought Holroyd.

Progress was rapid, but after a while, Holroyd began to sweat in the heat, and the shoulder straps of his backpack began to chafe. He took a tiny sip from his water bottle to ward off dehydration thinking he had no idea how long before he could replenish it with water safe to drink.

Juanito stayed close to Holroyd, and Holroyd tried talking to the boy though without much hope Juanito would understand. Perhaps a friendly tone would reassure the boy, but each time he tried to chat, one of the guards would yell "No talk!" and push Holroyd with the butt of his rifle.

As they proceeded, Holroyd guessed the time of day and the direction by the sun's position. Roughly estimating the speed of progress, he estimated the distance travelled so that by backtracking to their point of departure could be roughly located. *If we survive to do so.*

As before, the sounds of animals in the undergrowth could be heard occasionally, and often, brightly coloured birds startled by the party's approach flew away.

On one occasion, a troop of monkeys looked down at the party, and some began throwing fruit, at which one of the guards unslung his rifle and fired a couple of shots without hitting anything. Holroyd and Juanito flinched at the sound, and Juanito grasped Holroyd's hand for assurance.

"Idiota, ¿quieres que todas sepan que estamos aquí?" the guard's companion snarled. Holroyd understood that to mean a reproof for possibly calling attention to their presence.

"¿Quién está ahí para escucharnos? Cualquiera por aquí sabrá que somos nosotros y se mantendrá alejado." Holroyd thought his companion dismissed the reproof in a jeering tone. The party continued in silence, finally arriving at the stele.

Holroyd motioned to one of the men to use his machete and clear away the vegetation covering the mound. The man refused and gave the machete to Holroyd to get busy while he stood by with his rifle at the ready. Soon, the object's outlines underneath the mound revealed more of the rectangular tablet with incised script.

Holroyd stood looking at the tablet with mounting excitement. *Hopefully, the script will reveal who visited and when and how this stele is connected to Zhou man*

"Bueno, professor, ¿es esto lo que estaba buscando?" asked the senior of his guards.

"Is this what you look for?" the second guard translated.

"Yes," replied Holroyd, "I think so." He continued to scrape away lichen and take pictures. As he continued to remove vegetation and lichen, he exposed more of the tablet to reveal a four-sided obelisk with symbols on each side. *This is better than I had hoped for. It looks as if there are enough inscriptions to have recorded a lengthy narrative.* Excited by the idea, he ignored his increasing tiredness and discomfort from the heat and increased his pace of discovery.

Suddenly, the leading guard sat up, grabbed his gun, and gave an order to his companion, who also grabbed his gun, and both looked toward the edge of the clearing. Juanito grabbed Holroyd's arm as if seeking protection from something.

Holroyd was surprised but stopped work, wondering what had caused his guards to react. He heard the sound of something coming through the jungle, and by the sound, it seemed large. Juanito moaned and held Holroyd tighter.

Suddenly, four men with guns at the ready came out of the jungle but stopped, looking at the scene. Before anyone could say anything, Holroyd's guards fired at the men, hitting one who dropped his gun but did not fall. The men returned with rapid-fire that instantly killed the two guards and then looked at Holroyd and Juanito, who stood there trembling with fear.

Holroyd recognised the men as Chinese and holding Juanito close and yelled, *"Wǒmen shì péngyǒumen, qǐng bāngzhù wǒmen."*

The squad leader looked at Holroyd and replied, "I am so sorry, but your Chinese is terrible, and I did not understand. Please to repeat in English."

"We're friends, please help us."

"And why should we do so?"

"Because I am Peter Holroyd and this is my local assistant, Juanito."

"That is not interesting to me," retorted the squad leader.

"Wait," Holroyd hurriedly said. "You must be from the mine. Ask your manager, Wang Su about me, and he will confirm who I am."

"That is inconvenient. I prefer simple tasks, and by executing you two, this incident will be closed."

"And how will you explain your wounded companion?" asked Holroyd.

"That will be of no consequence and shouldn't worry you because you will be addressing your honourable ancestors."

One of the other men began to fidget and addressed the squad leader in a tone suggesting he wanted to know what was happening.

A conversation in Chinese followed that Holroyd did not understand, but at the end, the leader turned to Holroyd and said, "We will take you back with us."

As they went back, Holroyd asked the squad leader, "How is it that you arrived as you did?"

"After bandits attacked the mine, squads were sent to patrol the neighbourhood to find their nest and eradicate any danger of more attacks. We heard gunfire and came to investigate and found you by chance."

"Doctor, Holroyd! You're back again?" Wang Su looked up in surprise. "I was unaware our hospitality was so appealing." He turned to the squad leader, and a spate of Chinese followed.

Holroyd and Juanito returned to the camp with their rescuers where their return was greeted with surprise.

"Welcome back," Wang Su said, "Although I did not expect to see you again." And he turned to the squad leader.

After a lengthy conversation, Wang Su turned back to Holroyd and said, "Hu Man has briefed me on what happened. I confess your situation is more difficult than I appreciated. I will consult with Beijing, but until then, you are welcome here, but please do your best to remain inconspicuous."

"Thank you. That is most generous of you," Holroyd replied. "And the boy?"

"Ah, yes, the boy." Wang Su turned to Juanito and engaged in a lengthy conversation that Holroyd could not follow. In the end, Wang Su nodded, gave instructions to one of his men, and turned to Holroyd.

"I asked the boy if he knew anything about the bandits, but he is reluctant to talk about them," Wang Su reported.

"He should go home," Holroyd observed, and Wang Su nodded. Juanito left with an armed escort, and Holroyd retired to his quarters.

He looked at the photographs he had taken at the stele and wondered how he might get help in deciphering what he had found. Thinking over whom he might ask, he remembered a colleague in Taiwan, though he could not recall how to make contact without access to his computer. He wondered if Wang Su might be able to help him.

He went over to Wang Su and explained what he wanted, but that he only had his colleague's name and the institution at which he worked. Wang Su nodded and, downloading the pictures from Holroyd's phone, agreed to send them.

He reported success and that a reply had been received in which the colleague expressed great interest in the find, but that the pictures were not clear enough to permit decryption.

Holroyd thought over what he had learned. *I need to return and get better pictures, but how can I do that without endangering myself and anyone who might be prepared to accompany me?*

Holroyd opened his cell phone only to find it needed charging. He managed to borrow a charger from one of the miners who owned an iPhone. He used the interval to bathe, get some food, and rest. Tired as he was, sleep did not come, and after a while, he got up and checked the charge on his phone. He tried calling Wen Mei Li and Merry, but neither answered. He left messages asking them to call and lay down on his bed and, this time, fell asleep.

Chapter 36

Jimenez returned to his office and knocked on the *Jefe's* door.

"There's a report of smugglers using one of the villages up the coast, I'm going to investigate." The *Jefe* looked at him but finally nodded before returning to the papers on his desk.

Jimenez motioned his two trusted men to follow him, and together, they left, heading out of town. As their car sped through the streets, one of the men suddenly remarked. "*Teniente,* this is not the way to the village of the smugglers! Where are we going and why?"

"We're going to the pueblo near where the archeological team was massacred. I want to look around and see if we can find anything that wasn't reported to or by the team that's investigating the attack."

Once arrived at the pueblo, they stopped aghast at the scene they encountered. Bodies were lying in the street, and several houses were aflame. Jimenez immediately called for reinforcements and then, realizing his team's inadequacy to assist, started to determine the extent of the damage and who had been the attackers.

He approached one sobbing woman who was holding a bleeding man, presumably her husband.

He knelt to feel for the man's pulse and then shook his head.

"*Lo siento mucho, pero no hay nada que puedas hacer*," he said softly at which point the woman screamed and started wailing, rocking back and forth. "Nothing you can do but bury and mourn him," Jimenez muttered in English.

He looked around, noting how many similar scenes he could see. His men returned from their own observations and reported not only murders but atrocities indicating the brutality of the attack.

"Did you find out anything?" he asked his men.

"Bandits from the cartel, and something about revenge for revealing their activities," reported one of the men.

"Who revealed that?" asked Jimenez.

"A boy named Juanito."

"And where is he now?"

"He and his family were the first to be killed," the man reported, "and the bandits were particularly nasty about how they killed them. They killed the others and set the fires as a warning to keep quiet about the bandits and provide help when told to."

Knowing the attack fitted other cartel attacks across the country, Jimenez was not surprised at

what he was told. But this had happened in his back-
yard, which angered him, and he resolved to take
whatever action he could to ensure those responsible would never dare to try again. He and his men
returned to the city without waiting for the reinforcements.

Chapter 37

Holroyd woke to the ringing of the phone, and, on answering, he noted he had slept through two previous calls, one from Wen Mei Li and one from Merry. This call was from Wen Mei Li.

"Peter, I warned you not to live in interesting times," she said, "but it appears you did not heed my advice." She paused. "However, I am relieved that you are safe. Please tell me what happened."

Holroyd told her of his experiences, and then "I was surprised that Li Feng became so interested in the stele. I was unaware that Zhou Man or someone else may have buried treasure nearby."

"That is of no concern to me, even if it is to you," Wen Mei Li replied. "Can you tell me anything about the location of this wasps' nest where these bandits might be hiding?"

"Based on the time it took for us to get from their lair and the general direction in which we moved, I think we could backtrack and identify a general location that would narrow an area worth searching," Holroyd replied and gave the details. Wen Mei Li acknowledged the information and with a caution to take care, ended the call.

***

Wen Mei Li called Merry and gave an update.

"Peter is safe for the moment at our mine, but I think we should bring him to a safer place."

"I agree," Merry replied, "but short of sending the SAS in, I don't have any suggestions now."

"I can't ask our people there to do more than they already have. Do you have any contact that might help?"

"I can try, but it would be risky. The problem is we would need men we can trust, and they are difficult to locate. But perhaps we should look outside the local area, possibly Mexico City itself."

"Are you suggesting there are people who could be appropriately pressured?"

"Yes, but unfortunately, I don't have the contacts," Merry lied. *I hope that will be enough to keep Song safe.*

"I'll get back to you."

Merry sat back and considered his next move. He recognized if the warning was real; he was constrained in what he could do if he wanted to keep Song safe.

At the same time, he could not just shrug off the habits gained over a lifetime of loyal government service, nor did he feel he could abandon Holroyd to his fate without at least an effort to save him. He needed to do something proactive. He called Jimenez and asked for help.

Chapter 38

Jimenez considered what Merry asked him to do. Bringing Holroyd from the mine entailed dangers, not the least of which was possible interference by the cartel.

He debated putting together an armed escort but didn't know who he could trust to keep the task secret and approve the needed manpower. On the other hand, his two trusted men might be sufficient if he could get approval for them to investigate one of the many crimes outside the city but drive to the mine instead. On deciding to use the subterfuge, he obtained approval from the *Jefe* to proceed.

Once out of the city, progress was swift until rounding a corner, the road was blocked by a truck skewed across both lanes. Jimenez went over to see what had caused the truck to block the road and discovered that it had collided with an overturned farmer's tractor and trailer. Chickens were running loose, and several carcasses were strewn over the tarmac. The farmer and a couple of women quarrelled with the truck driver, and no one seemed concerned that traffic was blocked.

Jimenez strode over to the group and, in a loud voice, ordered them to clear the road and then give statements to his men. His arrival was greeted with surprise, but noting his uniform, the men set about moving their vehicles as best they could. Jimenez's men came over to help.

Meanwhile, the women clustered around Jimenez and clamoured to accuse the truck driver of causing the accident and demanding compensation for the loss of the livestock and income. Jimenez fended the women off with a barked order to desist but noticed the farmer and the driver whispering while glancing at him. *They're probably neighbours, and I don't like how they look at me. I'll have to watch out because they've probably got friends among one of the cartels I could be in greater danger than I already am if I'm identified. But then, what else is new?*

Once the road was cleared, Jimenez arrived at the camp and collected Holroyd, who was given a shabby hat and shirt and told to hunch down as far as he could in the back seat. Any casual observer watching the car go by could think some criminal had just been arrested and was being taken to jail.

The ruse worked because the car arrived safely and stopped outside a building in front of which a Mexican flag flapped lazily from a flagpole.

"This is a government audit office staffed by people I know and can trust," Jimenez informed Holroyd. "Please enter the front door with my men and pass through to the back door, where I will collect you and take you to a safe place owned and run by my family."

Holroyd was bundled out of the car into the building in a manner that supported the fiction that an arrested criminal was being handled roughly.

Neither the policemen nor Holroyd noticed Mickie sitting at a café table on the opposite side of the road.

Mickie sipped her Oaxaca *cafecito,* nibbled at a small pastry, and read the headlines of the English-language newspaper. The huge headline read 'Massacre at village' and was followed by a lurid report with photographs.

The article then reminded readers of the attack on the Chinese mine before declaiming, 'Enough is enough, and we demand authorities finally take action against these bandits.' *What attack on a Chinese mine? I don't remember reading about that.*

Appalled by the atrocity at the village, her journalistic instincts clicked in. *The cartel has attacked the archeological site, the Chinese mine, and now this village. All this happened after Holroyd arrived here and he was at the site. So, is Holroyd somehow present or even involved in the attacks on the mine and the village? If so, he must be very important in the drug trade. I wonder whom to ask.*

Mickie looked away from the paper across the street and saw how the police manhandled someone into a government building. With a start, she recognized Holroyd. *They've arrested Holroyd! This is the proof of his involvement in drugs that I've been looking for.*

Excited, she searched for her camera and stood up for a better view. By the time she was ready to take pictures, Holroyd and his escort had disappeared, and the car in which they had arrived had driven off.

Frustrated, she grabbed her bag, paid for her coffee and, narrowly avoiding a bus and a motorcycle that came careening down the road, ran across to enter the building where Holroyd had been taken. She entered a spacious hall with a reception booth to one side.

The receptionist looked up in surprise.

"Si señora, ¿puedo ayudarla?"

"Do you speak English?" Mickie went over to him. The receptionist shook his head, motioned to Mickie to wait, and picked up his phone.

A few minutes later, a man approached Mickie and said, "May I help you, lady?"

"Yes," Mickie replied breathlessly, "I just saw the police bring a man in here and want to know more."

"The police?" the man asked, puzzled. "Why would the police bring someone here? This is a federal government accounting office, and the police have no business here."

"Look, I saw the police come here," Mickie insisted.

The man looked at Mickie before turning to the receptionist and asking for confirmation. Then he turned back to Mickie.

"Josef says other than yourself and a delivery boy, only employees have entered this morning," he reported. "I regret, lady, but you are mistaken."

"Bullshit!" Mickie retorted. "Stop stonewalling. I demand to see for myself if they are here."

"That I cannot permit," the man advised. "But who are you to even make such a demand?"

"I am a Canadian journalist." Mickie pulled out her ID.

"Journalists are not permitted to enter here," the man replied, "and especially not foreign journalists. Now please leave before I call the police to remove you."

"Oh sure," Mickie retorted, "call the police! I have no doubt that, like the rest of the local police they can be relied upon to do as you want."

"Lady, you have that wrong," the man observed, "the local police have no authority here. If you refuse to leave, I shall call the *Federales*, and they will remove you and perhaps even arrest you for trespassing on federal property." He stopped. "Is that clear?"

Mickie realised she was not getting anywhere and left. *Perhaps Strang will be more cooperative.*

Strang was not overjoyed at Mickie's visit. He agreed to meet her only when it was obvious she was not about to leave without seeing him.

"Well?' he asked. "What now?"

"Have you any comment about Holroyd's arrest?"

"Come again," Strang sat up as if stung. "Is this another wet dream of yours or do you have proof?"

"You didn't know?" Mickie enjoyed knowing something Strang did not and told him what she had witnessed. Strang looked at her in silence.

"Looks as if you've got yourself a scoop," he said grudgingly. "Thanks for letting me know."

"Any comments? "Mickie persisted.

"Nope," Strang replied. "Now get going!"

Mickie was out of the office before he reached for his phone.

"We have to meet," he said, "Holroyd's here."

"That is interesting," the person answered, "I suggest you apprehend him or, failing that, make sure he never leaves."

Chapter 39

Philip finished his morning coffee and decided it was time to make his pastoral rounds again. He should find out what had been arranged for the funeral of the fishermen who had agreed to ferry himself and Holroyd to the stele but had died in the collision at sea.

He wandered through familiar streets greeting and chatting with several of his parishioners when he passed a cantina he occasionally visited. He noted several clients on the terrace, including one of the community leaders he wanted to talk to.

He was about to enter when he noticed the *Jefe* at a table with someone else inside, apparently deep in conversation. The *Jefe's* companion was partially hidden behind a corner, and Philip could not see enough to identify who it might be.

A waiter Philip knew as one of the black sheep in his flock came out to serve customers on the terrace and, noticing Philip, waved. Philip waved back and beckoned the man to come over.

"Hola, José," Philip smiled

"Brother Philip, welcome back." José profusely shook Philip's hand.

Indicating the man and the *Jefe,* Philip asked, "José, have you overheard anything those two are talking about?"

"Brother Philip," José protested, "I do not do such a thing."

"Of course not," Philip agreed, "but sometimes you cannot help but hear things not meant for your ears. Perhaps on this occasion?"

"Not yet," José answered and winked before going back inside.

Philip sauntered away from the cantina to avoid attracting attention from the unknown man or the *Jefe.* He returned only when he thought they would have left. When he arrived, they had gone, and he went in and ordered a beer.

"I did not hear very much," José reported, "they seemed uneasy and often looked around the cantina as if watching for someone. I heard them say something about a problem that needed immediate correction. I heard the word 'disappear,' but that's all."

"Do you know to what or whom they were referring?"

"No." José shrugged his shoulders.

"Anything else? "Philip asked, but José only looked at him and grinned slyly.

"Come on, José," Philip said encouragingly, "You know I return favours."

"Sí," José nodded. "There was a name. Some-one called Orod, I think."

"Could it have been Holroyd?"

"Perhaps yes," José nodded.

"And that is all you heard?"

"Yes," José nodded.

"I won't forget this," Philip said and stood up. "Thank you, José. Give my greetings to Josephina and the kids." And he left.

***

"Brother Philip," Mickie called out as Philip was about to enter his home. "You've been hiding, but now I've caught up with you."

Philip turned to see who was addressing him and frowned when he saw Mickie. He considered entering and closing the door behind him without meeting her but decided he'd better listen to what she had to say.

"Well," he said, "now you have. What is it you want this time?"

"Have you any comment about Holroyd's arrest?" Mickie asked.

"What about his arrest?" Philip asked, suddenly worried.

Mickie explained what she had seen. *Did that man and the police chief solve their problem by arresting Peter? If so, to whom can I turn for help?* He looked at Mickie.

"How do you know for sure that it was Holroyd?"

"Believe me," Mickie answered. "I always make sure of something before I go further."

"And just what was the charge?" Philip asked.

"I think you know very well what the charge was," Mickie retorted. "He's up to his nose in the drug traffic."

Philip silently looked at her before asking, "Where do you come from, again?"

"Canada," she answered proudly.

"I think you forgot to bring your brains with you," Philip said and entered his house, slamming the door behind him.

"You've had your chance, Philip," he heard her yell through the door. *So have you, young lady. I think you'll be reconsidering your future long before*

I'll need to think about mine. I wonder who the chief of police was talking to.

He believed Mickie's report that Holroyd had been arrested but was worried if the arresting officers were local or federal. *"If the locals have him, I might get some information from Jimenez, but if it's the Federales, I don't know whom to call."* He tried to call Jimenez but was unable to reach him.

Chapter 40

Mickie opened the newspaper, frustrated that so much foreign news was always a day or two after the event. Not, however, in this addition. On page one, the headline was not only up to date but also impossible to miss: 'China to send Chinese army to protect local mine.'

She focused on the article and read that China demanded reparations for the attack on the mine and higher security for the future. If the Mexican Government could or would not meet these demands, China would consider sending in its military to protect the lives of its citizens and its property. Should that not be possible, China would have no alternative but to cancel the contract and demand cancellation charges.

In a later report, the Mexican Government regretted the tone of the demands but agreed to send in its army and wipe out the bandits.

Mickie put down the paper. *That will ruffle a few feathers. Can the army be trusted? Let me see what Strang has to say.*

Strang was in no mood to spend time chatting with Mickie, but he did let her know that, in his opinion, the matter could have been left to the local authorities to deal with. He refused any further comments and bid her a curt dismissal.

***

"*Hola prima, hemos encontrado el nido de los bandidos y estamos entrando para acabar con él. Sé que estás interesado por lo que pasó en el pueblo, así que puedes venir extraoficialmente.*" Jimenez jumped at the offer. He called his men.

"The army has found the bandits' nest, and we've been unofficially invited to go with them to destroy it."

The attack was brutal, but in the end, only a few wounded bandits were left to surrender. Several corpses had been thrown onto a heap while, next to it, a couple of soldiers were hurriedly digging a communal grave.

The metallic smell of blood was mixing with the lingering smells of cordite and defecation. To add to the unpleasantness, swarms of flies were already crawling over the bodies and buzzing around an annoying the sweating men.

One of the young soldiers was off to one side vomiting copiously. Jimenez looked at him, feeling regret. *It's terrible, but unfortunately, you'll see it again and maybe get used to it. Perhaps we'll live to see the day when hunting down vermin won't be necessary.*

The captured men sat in the hot sun as a group, hands tied behind their backs. Their wounds were left unattended and attracted insects that added to their misery. However, they maintained defiant attitudes, often yelling insults at the soldiers who responded by using their rifle butts to deliver painful blows.

Jimenez and his men watched the proceedings emotionlessly, sometimes passing comments amongst themselves that could be taken as approval. Meanwhile, the camp was searched.

One group reported finding a laboratory that was then demolished in a huge explosion that rained debris on the prisoners and guards alike.

Another group found communications equipment and a trove of documents that were handed to the captain for him to look at. After reading several documents, he called Jimenez.

"Come and look at these emails," he said. "I think you'll be interested in some of these names."

Jimenez went over the documents.

"De Falta?" he exclaimed. "He's our local police chief, but I know nothing of this Li. But perhaps one of the prisoners will cooperate and tell us more." He then asked. "With your permission?" The captain agreed, and Jimenez nodded at his men.

The captain and Jimenez ignored the sounds of blows and groans but continued to look over the documents together.

"The man Li is a China man," one of the men reported to Jimenez, "full name Li Feng. He was here giving orders."

"Li Feng?" asked Jimenez, "are you sure that's that name?"

"*Si, teniente*," the man said.

"Is there a Chinese man among the prisoners, or did anyone find a dead one?" Jimenez turned to the captain, who in turn asked his Sergeant, only to get a negative shake of the head.

"I think that's something for you to handle," the captain addressed Jimenez. "We'll just finish cleaning up here."

Jimenez reviewed the day's events as he drove back to the city. *Thank goodness we cleaned out that nest of brigands, but at what cost? How many families have been ruined by these people, and to what end? And how much longer will this go on?*

He sighed and changed his thoughts to ponder about this Li Feng. *Who is this guy, and how is he involved with the bandits? I would like to know if Holroyd has any information. A talk with him might be useful.*

Chapter 41

Jimenez asked Holroyd what he knew of Li Feng and Holroyd and explained what he knew.

"Do you know where we might find him, or who might know?" Asked Jimenez.

"No," answered Holroyd, "but the boy Juanito might have some idea. Go ask him."

Jimenez looked at Holroyd, realising Holroyd had no idea of what had happened at Juanito's pueblo.

"I am sorry to have to tell you, but the bandits murdered Juanito along with his family and many others. It was not nice."

Holroyd was stunned and, turning pale had to sit down trembling.

"Oh, no!" he groaned with tears running down his cheeks. "That poor, poor boy. He didn't deserve this." He reached for a handkerchief and stayed silent while Jimenez looked on in sympathy.

Recovering somewhat from his initial grief, Holroyd wiped the tears from his face and looked at Jimenez.

"I want to attend his funeral," he said.

"Have you gone *loco*?" Jimenez was aghast. "Probably half the men in the district are looking to kidnap or kill you, and you want to go to a funeral that lots of people will attend."

"I owe it to him," said Holroyd defiantly. "The boy deserves it."

"I won't agree," replied Jimenez. "this is, how you say it? Ah! Yes! A pure folly! There is no way I can guarantee your safety."

"I don't think you can stop me," Holroyd replied, "but there is another factor you might want to consider."

"And that is?" Jimenez asked doubtfully.

"Li Feng is probably still alive and thinks I can give him something he badly wants," Holroyd said. "He's not about to harm me as long he continues to think that way."

"Maybe not Li Feng," observed Jimenez. "But there are plenty of others."

"From what I can see, the others obey Li Feng for now," Holroyd said, "but that will stop when he thinks I can't do what he wants."

"Then make sure he doesn't come to that conclusion before you are out of his reach," retorted Jimenez drily. Holroyd could only nod in agreement.

"I still want to attend Juanito's funeral," Holroyd repeated.

Jimenez looked at him in consternation. "Have you any idea what danger you will put yourself in?" But before Holroyd could protest, Jimenez went on. "I couldn't guarantee your safety, and even if I thought I could, I don't have the resources."

"As I told you, I don't believe I'll be in danger," Holroyd retorted. "And even if there is any suggestion of a threat against me, I want to attend the boy's funeral. I owe him that, at least."

Jimenez shrugged his shoulders and looked at him silently before saying, "As you wish. I will ask my men to accompany you, but I won't order them. They may refuse."

Luckily for Holroyd, the men did not refuse.

On the way, the men explained that in Mexico, death is viewed as a stage in life, and folks tend to embrace rituals surrounding death more readily than in the rest of North America. Rather than rushing to bury the body, most families spend time with their deceased loved one in the house, mourning the loss.

During this time, people close to the deceased visit the home, hold night prayers, pass condolences, and give gifts of food or money. It is a time for all to eat, drink and reminisce together in grief.

Arriving at the village, Holroyd noted that people had already moved to the cemetery, which proved to be an area carved out of the jungle. Several mounds, some with an iron cross and some with a stone marker indicating who lay beneath the earth. Many had vases of fresh or withered flowers at the mound.

Several groups were gathered around different graves and upon asking, Holroyd and his escort were pointed at one site where a few people were gathered. Surprised, the mourners looked at the new arrivals, but a few nodded in greeting.

Holroyd felt tears running down his cheeks as he surveyed the pitifully small grave that held Juanito's body. *What a terrible, terrible waste.* Holroyd stood there, silently offering a prayer for Juanito's soul.

A couple of bunches of flowers had been placed at the grave's edges and a wreath to which a label was attached. Holroyd moved to be able to read the label and found Li Feng had sent it. *So Li Feng observes the Chinese custom of niceties of funerals, respecting the dead even when he was the cause of the death.* Suddenly, he felt someone clasp his arm and turned to see who it was.

Next to him stood a swarthy man dressed in mourning black, looking at the grave and holding a small wreath. *Probably one of the mourners, but why the clasp?* The man bent down to place the wreath by the grave and stood up with bowed head.

He shuffled closer to Holroyd and without looking at Holroyd, the man said, "*Señor* Li Feng sends his condolences but reminds you not to forget your agreement with him. He is not a very patient man and can be very cruel if he does not get what he wants from people. He will be in touch with you soon." And the man turned and left without another word.

Holroyd sighed. *Li Feng likely calculated I might turn up here and inevitably contact me. But at least it supports that he won't do anything as long as he thinks I will give him what he wants.*

He stood by the grave for a while longer and then said, "I have something I must do before we return to the city."

"*Senor*?" his escort asked.

"I need to photograph the stele. Li Feng has my phone with the photographs, and I will need my own for a better examination if I'm to answer Li Feng."

The escort looked at each other and finally shrugged in agreement. Holroyd passed on his condolences to the other mourners, went to the stele to take its photographs, and returned to the city.

Chapter 42

Mickie answered the call from Breckenridge with some worry. *What will I say if he asks me where I am on my research?*

"Hello, Mickie," Breckenridge greeted her. "I hope I'm not dragging you away from the beach, but I am waiting for your report. How is that going?"

"It looks as if I'm right," Mickie replied. "Holroyd is up to his neck in the drugs trade, but I don't yet know fully what his role is." And she went to report what she had seen and learned. "I'm writing it up and should have it to you by tomorrow. But you can call Strang for corroboration."

"Strang?" asked the Count. "Who is he?"

"I'm not sure what his role is," Mickie answered, "but I think he's the American man following the Mexican drug business." She thought for a moment. "He probably has other duties."

"Such as?"

"He might be CIA, but I don't know." She hesitated. "Anyway, here's the number you can call him."

"I'll do that, but you can start writing." And the call ended.

The article duly appeared under a blaring front-page headline. 'Drug Kingpin Professor.'

In Vancouver, Simon O'Mallory smiled in satisfaction. *That should put you in your place and vindicate your colleagues at the university.* He continued to read again, savouring each sentence.

'Peter Holroyd, once a visiting professor here at our university, has been revealed as an important link in the chain that binds the Chinese and Mexican drug trade. Holroyd was present when a local drug cartel massacred an archeological team for being too close for comfort. Subsequently, he was complicit in planning a massacre at a nearby village the inhabitants of which had revealed the location of the cartel's nearby base.'

Heart-wrenching details of the atrocities were included throughout the article. The article continued, 'The local police have since arrested Holroyd although authorities who had provided corroborative information remained unnamed because they were not authorised to make comments. It is expected that Holroyd will appear in court soon to answer the charges. If found guilty, Holroyd will face a lengthy jail sentence.'

Chapter 43

Holroyd returned home, and as he started to unpack, the front door opened, and Sean walked in.

"Hello, father." Sean smiled, but Holroyd could see he was tired.

"Welcome back," Holroyd answered and went over to give his son a big hug. "How was your trip?"

"Not quite what I had hoped for," Sean replied, and he dropped his rucksack on the floor.

"How so?" Holroyd stepped back.

Sean gave a short description of the trip and the disaster that had befallen the others in his group. Holroyd silently looked at this son before saying, "That is terrible. Those poor people and their families." He stopped. "Thank goodness you are safe."

"If I hadn't returned, Mother would have thrown a fit," Sean said with a weak grin. Before Holroyd could say anything, Sean asked, "What have you been doing while I was away?"

"I went down to Mexico," Holroyd said. Seeing a puzzled frown on Sean's face, he went on, "I went to look for a stele that might have been placed there by early Chinese explorers."

"Did you find it?"

"Yes, and it might be what I hoped to find," Holroyd said. He took out his phone and showed the pictures he had taken.

Sean looked at them and was about to return the phone but had another closer look.

"Can you read what's written there?" he asked. Holroyd shook his head.

Again, Sean looked at the photos and said, "Can I have copies? I want to play with them on my hologram producer. Holroyd nodded.

"But not now," he said. "We both need to relax and recover from our travels. Go and unpack and we'll go out for dinner."

Sean went to his room, and Holroyd returned to unpacking when the phone rang. It was Wen Mei Li, and she expressed her disappointment at the article.

"What article?" asked Holroyd.

"You haven't read it?" Wen Mei Li asked, sounding surprised. "Then I think you should do so as quickly as possible."

Before he could promise, she hung up, but the phone rang again immediately.

"Peter!" Pearl's voice barrelled down the line. "You promised not to get involved in dangerous activities while I was away. You told me …"

"I didn't." Holroyd interrupted as forcefully as he thought he could get away with.

"Don't you dare lie to me," Pearl barked, and Holroyd realised he was in deep trouble.

"Darling," he said but got no further.

"Don't you darling me!" Pearl yelled. "You are lying, and I have seen the newspaper that tells me so."

"Whatever is in that newspaper is a lie," Holroyd protested. "Go and talk to Wen Mei Li. She will confirm it." There was silence.

"Don't leave home again."

The line went dead. *I won't dear. You can take that to the bank. I'd better get a copy of the newspaper and see what all the fuss is about.* The phone rang again.

"Peter, old boy," Merry's voice floated down the line. "Have you been a naughty boy?"

"Don't be ridiculous, Merry," Holroyd protested. "You know me better than that."

"Unless you've been pulling the wool over my eyes, I do," Merry answered seriously. "But that doesn't help very much. That article has roused sleeping dogs, and a simple denial won't quite do the trick in getting them back to sleep. What do you know of the journalist, and just who might these un-named sources be?"

"The journalist works for the Victoria newspaper. She contacted me before I went to Mexico and told me was doing some investigative work on the movement of drugs from Asia to Mexico. She also asked about Sean, but I don't know why. I next met her in Mexico at De Perrefalta's reception, which surprised me. I did notice she seemed to be in contact with the American man on the spot, Strang, but again, I don't know why."

"Anything else?"

"The local police chief might have had some input. Jimenez told me he isn't the upstanding police chief people would like to have." Merry was silent.

"Let me see what can be done," Merry said finally. "Meanwhile, try and become inconspicuous, would you?"

"I'll do my best," Holroyd promised "But there is a complication." He went on to explain his predicament with Li Feng.

"I see," Merry said. After a moment, he went on. "Have you corroborated what he thinks is on the stele?"

"No," Holroyd said, "I have to do more research."

"Then fob him off with that," Merry said. "And in the meantime, I would suggest you not stay in touch and follow my advice to lie low."

"That may not be so easy," Holroyd answered. "He suspects I know more than I do."

"Let him suspect all he wants, old boy," Merry retorted. "It's not your main concern now. Focus on the safety of you and your family." And he hung up. *Thanks, Merry, very helpful advice, that is.*

The door opened and Sean stood there with a big smile on his face.

"I put your photos through my producer and come and see what the preliminary results are." He took Holroyd by the arm and went together to Sean's room.

On a tabletop was what Holroyd considered a collection of instruments, none of which he recognised. However, the centrepiece was a holographic reproduction of the stele on which several inscriptions were recognisable. Holroyd peered at the inscriptions and recognized the name Zhou Man and references to both trade and gold.

"Well done," Holroyd exclaimed and slapped Sean on the back. "This helps enormously, but we're not there yet."

"What do you need?" asked Sean,

"The inscription mentions Zhou Man," Holroyd answered, "but we don't yet know if Zhou Man was on board or is mentioned in another way. Furthermore, the references to trade and gold don't tell us whether they traded goods for gold or brought gold to trade for goods. And, finally, we don't know if the stele records that they left for home." He stopped. "Do you think you could work on what you have to see if we can get further information?"

"Not here," Sean said, "I'd have to go over to the lab and see what we can do."

"We?" asked Holroyd.

"I'll need my team on this."

"Can they be trusted not to discuss this with anyone not part of the team?"

"Oh, yes."

Sean was confident and Holroyd nodded his agreement.

Chapter 44

"Peter." Philip sounded agitated. "There's terrible news! There was an ambush, and Jimenez was killed along with half a dozen other policemen."

"Oh, no!" Holroyd was shocked and saddened by the news. "He was a good and honourable man. Many people will sorely miss him. Do we know what happened?"

"All I read is that a small contingent of policemen was going to a village where smugglers were reported to be. They were ambushed on the way. However, some of my flock have told me it had to have been planned with advance notice because of where and how the ambush took place."

"But who would do such a thing?" asked Holroyd.

"Rumour has it that the police chief is involved," answered Philip.

"Surely, he would not have been that stupid to have been involved directly," observed Holroyd.

"It's well known he had no love for Jimenez," said Philip. "If he is involved, it would also explain the particular brutality they used to execute Jimenez. He was tortured and then slowly murdered." Philip stopped and then said, "It was barbaric."

There was silence until Holroyd asked, "What about Jimenez's family? I think something should be done to help them."

"I agree," replied Philip. "I'll pass the word to my flock. Hopefully, someone will do something, but given the threat these thugs present, I'm not sure anyone will."

"But surely…" Holroyd stopped, recognising the futility of anything he could say. "Thanks for the news, but honestly, I wish you had not been in the position to have to pass on such a horrifying report." He stopped, before adding, "What will it take to stop all this misery?"

"Stopping all the corruption would be a good first step," Philip observed. "But good luck on that." And the call ended.

Holroyd sat back, overcome with feelings of sorrow, helplessness, and outrage. *There has to be something I can do. Surely, there are ways to punish those responsible, perhaps starting with the police chief and maybe Strang, but including Li Feng. I'm sure they are in this together. But how is the question? Perhaps Merry knows a way or even Wen Mei Li. I think they owe me that.*

He got up, poured himself a stiff drink and tried unsuccessfully to reach Merry but had to settle for a 'call me back' message instead.

Chapter 45

"Your Grace," the footman stood at the door waiting for Merry's acknowledgement.

"Yes?" Merry looked up from the paper on his desk and looked at the man.

"There's a policeman to see you," reported the man.

"I gave orders that I was not to be disturbed," Merry answered in an irritated voice. "Did he say what it's about?"

"No, your Grace." The man shifted as if nervous. "Only that it was of a personal nature."

"I see," said Merry. "Well, show him in."

"Inspector Watkins, Your Grace." The policeman introduced himself. "I'm in charge of the station that covers the local area, including the Estate."

"You must be new, then," said Merry. "I thought Inspector Jones was in charge."

"No, sir. Inspector Jones had to take early retirement for health reasons."

"I see," said Merry. "How may I help you? I assume you haven't come here only to introduce yourself."

"No sir, I haven't," Watkins said. "It concerns the young gentleman who I believe resides with your Grace."

"What about him?"

"I'm sorry to have to report he was brutally attacked and has been sent to hospital with some serious injuries," Watkins reported.

Merry turned white as if he'd been poleaxed and almost lost his balance, but Watkins moved forward and stopped a fall. Gently, he led Merry to a nearby leather wingback chair, and Merry collapsed into it.

"Be so kind as to pour me a brandy," Merry croaked and waved towards a sideboard on which were several decanters and glasses. "Help yourself, if you like."

"Thank you, no, sir," Watkins replied as he went over to the sideboard. "I'm on duty." He poured a stiff drink and handed it to Merry who took a deep draught. There was silence for a moment.

"Which hospital?" Merry asked.

"The Holy Trinity, sir."

"Where is that?" Merry asked.

"I can drive you over," Watkins said. "I have to go there and see what I can learn about the incident." He hesitated. "However, I doubt the young man will be in any state to make a statement."

"That would be most helpful of you." Merry got out of his chair and somewhat unsteadily walked to the bell to summon a footman. Once the man arrived, Merry informed the man that he was going to the hospital and gave instructions that his car should come to collect him when summoned. Furthermore, his mother was to be informed that Song was indisposed but she would be kept up to date as soon as more information became available.

Once at the hospital, they were taken to the ICU, but not permitted to enter Song's room. Merry had a sudden and unaccustomed feeling of panic. *Is it that serious?* Looking through the glass, Merry could see that Song was in traction and heavily bandaged. As he stood there, a doctor came up to him.

"Your Grace?" the doctor addressed Merry. "Do you know the next of kin? I think they should be informed."

Merry felt as if he'd been punched in the gut. *Oh, dear God, please let Song recover. Don't take him away from me.* And then managed to reply, "I am all the next of kin he has. At least, all that I know of. He may have family in Thailand, but I have no idea how to reach them quickly."

"I see," the doctor said noncommittedly.

"What's his situation?" Merry asked.

"As you can see, sir," the doctor said. "He is in traction and has internal injuries. Just how serious those injuries are we don't yet know."

"When will you know?"

"Hopefully, in the next few hours."

"Please keep me informed," Merry requested. "And do whatever you have to do to make him better."

"Then I'm going to have to ask you to sign certain documents to give us the necessary authority."

Merry nodded and looked at Song again. Watkins came up to him.

"That's a sorry sight, sir," Watkins remarked. "I hope he will recover."

"Thank you, Inspector," Merry replied. "I hope so, too. Do we know what happened?"

"It seems the young man was walking down the street when a car came out of nowhere and hit him. It stopped and reversed over him, and two men jumped out. Witnesses say the men bent over the young man and gave him a few more blows before driving off. No one recorded the license plate, and the car's description isn't much help either." He reported. "I'd say the brutality of the attack suggests

228

the attackers knew whom they were attacking and had a reason to do so.”

“Damn these bastards,” Merry exclaimed. “Find them and bring them in for punishment.” Watkins nodded.

“There is one thing, sir.” Watkins went on and handed Merry a piece of paper. “This was found on the young man. I wonder if you can tell me what it’s about?”

Merry took the paper and read, ‘Please be so good as to honour our agreement.’ He handed the paper back to Watkins.

“Any idea to what agreement this refers?” asked Watkins.

“No, Inspector,” Merry replied, “none at all.” *Damn you, Cheng. When I get hold of you, I’ll see to it personally that you get hung, drawn, and quartered before anyone notices you’re missing.*

Chapter 46

"Peter, have you lost your senses?!" Merry sounded worried.

"I have no idea what you are referring to," Holroyd replied.

"I have been told there is an article on a website or in a journal to which your son contributes." Merry waited before asking. "Do you know about it? Because, in my humble opinion, it wasn't the best idea to go for publication. It's likely to attract all the wrong attention."

"Thanks, Merry." Holroyd became worried by the call. "No, I wasn't aware, but I'll find out." He hung up and phoned Sean.

"Sean, I just got a call about something on a website or in a journal you contribute to. What's that about?"

"Honest, Father," Sean replied in a tone that Holroyd wasn't sure if it was from embarrassment or panic. "I had nothing to do with that."

"With what exactly?"

"I'll give you the URL and read it for yourself," Sean said. "It's accessible only to subscribers, so use my logins. I will help clean and lock up here, and we should talk about it when I get home." The call ended, and shortly afterwards, Holroyd received a text with the URL

The headline read, 'Computer generated copies and translation of ancient carvings on Chinese stele to reveal the treasure's location.' The byline was under the name of Brain. *That's obviously a pseudonym probably used by one of Sean's team.*

He discovered that the article contained a detailed report of everything Holroyd had wanted to know but wanted to keep secret until an appropriate time.

He sat down, trembling and confused, fearful of the possible consequences. *If Li Feng manages to get hold of it, he will be furious. But what a stupid, stupid thing to have published. This puts me and probably them in danger. I have to warn them.*

He picked up his phone to call Sean, but there was no answer, so he left a message.

Chapter 47

Sean put down the phone and tried to think about the next step. He felt embarrassed that someone, probably on his team, had betrayed his father's trust. *Was it Rajeesh or Viktor? Should challenge them outright? If I do, that will be the end of the team because the guilty one will lie, and the innocent one will be upset both by the betrayal and by the suspicion of being guilty. And if someone else published, both will be upset, and the question is who that someone else is and how did they get the information.* He stopped. *The cat's already out of the bag, and I don't see any advantage to having a row with the others just yet.*

Having decided to wait before facing the others, he returned to the lab and helped put away and secure the equipment. Once completed, the three of them walked to the exit, and Sean detected no strained talk or shifty looks. *Whichever of them did it, is also an excellent actor.*

Reaching the front door, Sean paused to lock it, while Rajeesh and Viktor went down the front steps to the pavement and waited for him there. As they looked up at him, neither noticed a black van pull up behind them.

The side door of the van opened, and three men jumped out. Two grabbed Rajeesh before he could react and roughly pushed him into the van while the third man lunged at Viktor. Viktor was caught unawares and fell heavily to the ground, trying to break his fall with his hand. There was a snap as something broke and he screamed in pain.

The commotion was loud enough to cause Sean to turn away from the door to see what had caused it. Seeing the mayhem unfolding on the street, Sean yelled loudly, "Hey! What are you doing?"

The yell was loud enough that others on the street noticed and began converging on the van. The men in the van saw that they had attracted attention, slammed the door shut and drove off at speed.

By the time Sean got down to the pavement, several people were there, one attending to Viktor, who was sitting up but obviously in pain.

"I've called the police," someone said. Others wanted to know what had happened and who those men were.

Sean hunkered by Viktor. "How are you? Anything broken?"

"I think so," Viktor answered with a weak grin. "I just don't know all the places."

Sean nodded sympathetically. "Any idea what this is about?"

Viktor shook his head, even though the movement caused him pain. "I think they wanted all three of us," he said weakly. "Just your good luck to have been up there locking the door, or you might be in the van with Rajeesh."

Sean nodded. "This has to do with that damn article," he muttered.

"What article?" Viktor asked.

"We'll talk about that later." Sean avoided answering. "Right now, you've got to go and have yourself looked at, and I think I'm about to have a conversation with the police." *But I'm not sure what I can tell them.*

Chapter 48

Merry sat next to Song's bed and watched the slow breathing that might have been assisted by some of the medical instruments around the room. There was an irritating whine from somewhere, but he didn't know it was from inside or outside the room.

Looking around the spartan-like room, he could see monitors and tubes but had yet to learn what they were there for. It was an efficient, if soulless, room. The only relief came from the flowers from Merry's friends and tenants. But it suited Merry's mood.

Song's injuries were the message to Merry that Cheng was serious in demanding Merry fulfill their agreement and ruthless regarding reminders. But much as Merry wanted to protect Song, his Civil Service training honed by experience gained over thirty years demanded he refuse Cheng's request. He sat there trying to think his way out of the problem.

Just then, Song stirred. "Merry?" he said. "You're here!" He then reached for Merry's hand before saying, "Thank you so much." And he relapsed into unconsciousness.

Merry grasped Song's hand gently. Then stood up and planted a kiss before going out of the hospital.

As he was driven back to the estate, he phoned the Cabinet Secretary's office and asked for a meeting to be scheduled. The reply came that Sir John suggested lunch at their club.

Sir John was already at the bar when Merry arrived.

"Let's go right on in for lunch, Meredith," Sir John greeted Merry. "I had a feeling that we should have an unofficial chat first. One that will allow us to exchange our views freely, as it were, without putting it down in writing."

Over lunch, Merry explained that his new duties as the Duke and now Song's accident required all his attention and made it impossible for him to fulfill his obligations as a government official.

"I had a feeling that this is what you wanted to discuss," Sir John remarked. "And I've given it some thought, which I then raised with the PM." He stopped to take a sip of wine. He deliberately replaced the glass on the table and looked at Merry.

"We both feel it would be unfortunate if you were to step back at this stage." He paused to let the message sink in. "However, we can assist you in several ways." He then commented. "All of which should not be divulged in case others feel envious."

A slight smile touched his lips, and Merry knew him well enough to know Sir John had just made a joke. "I'm not sure...." Merry started, but Sir John interrupted him.

"Your mother, the Dowager Duchess, is quite capable of managing the estate affairs for a little while longer, which leaves what to do about young Song."

Merry sat up surprised. *Is nothing secret anymore?*

"Oh, Meredith," Sir John went on. "We are quite familiar with the situation, and it's not for us to judge. We propose expediting his citizenship and moving him to a secure location where we can protect him under a new name. What happens after we've managed to solve our drug problem can be decided at that time."

He took another sip of wine. "You will be given a secure place near the Cabinet Office, personal bodyguards and an increased budget. " He took another sip. "Unfortunately, you won't be able to pursue your club habits for the duration, but I think you will agree that is a minor inconvenience."

Merry nodded. *That's very decent of him and is probably the best solution.*

"There is one other factor we might have to consider." Sir John looked at Merry. "There was an incident that involved your friend Peter Holroyd. His son, or at least his son's associates, were attacked as they left their laboratory. We don't know what was behind it. Still, considering that article in the Canadian newspaper implying Holroyd is involved in the drugs business, you might want to consider distancing yourself from him until we can be sure he's clean."

"Oh don't be ridiculous, John," Merry said. "I've known Peter since we went to school together. There's no way he'd be involved in drugs." He stopped. "For one, his wife would castrate him if she even thought he might be involved." He dwelt on that before adding. "Anyway, I doubt he has enough brains for that."

"Really?" Sir John raised his eyebrows. "I hope you're correct because as far as I have been informed, you're very much in the minority." He put down his napkin and started to get up. "Just be very careful. This is becoming a far bigger issue than we realised originally, and the PM is getting concerned."

Merry rose and promised to do his best while mentally crossing his fingers. *Bloody pompous ass! There are enough bodies out there who believed the promises that he and his people could keep them safe. Not on my watch! I can do as well, if not better than they could, by keeping Song at home with my own people watching over his safety.* With those thoughts in his mind, Merry drove home. But halfway there, another thought struck him.

If I don't take advantage of the offer and step back as Cheng wants me to, I may find myself in his power forever, and there would be no guarantee that Song will be safer. No! I'll go along with the offer and do my darndest to bring Cheng and his people to heel. With that thought uppermost, he felt a lot more confident. *Now, what should I do about Peter Holroyd, and will he go along with anything I propose?*

Chapter 49

Holroyd and Sean were at home when the doorbell rang. Sean went to answer it and returned with two men who introduced themselves as Detective Inspector Manorford and Detective Sergeant Mason from the Metropolitan Police.

"How can I help you ?" asked Holroyd.

"We're following up on the abduction of Rajeesh Badashvami," said Manorford, "And just want to clarify a couple of matters."

"Certainly," Holroyd said. "Please, sit down, and let's see if I can help."

"Thank you, sir," Manorford replied. "Now, your son gave us a description of what happened. We also interviewed Viktor Shostakovich, who was injured in the attack." He turned to Sean. " He thought the attack was aimed at all three of you but was foiled when bystanders came to your aid." He asked, "Is that also your opinion?"

"I don't know," Sean answered. "I was too far away to really see what was happening."

"Then we are left with the question of whether the attack was aimed solely at Mr. Badashvami or at all three of you." Manorford paused. "Would you have any thoughts as to which scenario is more likely?"

Sean shook his head, whereupon Manorford looked at Holroyd, "And how about you, sir?"

"I'm sorry, Inspector," he said, " I have no answer either." *And certainly not for your ears, Inspector.*

"Aren't you the Peter Holroyd who was arrested in China for tomb robbing or something?" asked Mason. "And then arrested in Canada on suspicion of murder?"

"Yes, Sergeant," answered Holroyd, irritated by the questions. "As I am sure you will have found, I was cleared in both cases."

"Yes, sir. You were." Mason looked at Holroyd with an expressionless face. "But according to a Canadian newspaper, you are now involved in smuggling drugs out of Mexico." He stopped before adding. "You have just come back from Mexico, I believe."

Holroyd looked at the Sergeant and said in a tone of derision but also some wariness, "And you believe that article, do you?"

"I wouldn't say we believe it, sir," Manorford interjected. "But as I am sure you will agree, if the article is accurate, there is another possibility for the attack on the young gentlemen."

"Spell it out for me, please, Inspector," Holroyd requested.

"Perhaps, sir," Manorford explained, "you've been a naughty boy, and your associates are sending you a message that they don't approve of whatever you might or might not have done."

"That is the most asinine idea I have ever heard coming from the Met," Holroyd snorted.

"That may be so, sir," Manorford observed. "But we'll be looking at all possible explanations and keeping an open mind until we have something definite. Not planning on any out-of-country trips, are you, sir?"

"No, Inspector. Is there anything else?" Holroyd was irritated and just wanted the policemen to leave. The policemen stood up to go.

"No sir," Manorford said. "Thank you for your time, and please let us know if you have anything to add that will help us."

Sean showed them to the door before coming back to Holroyd.

"What article were they talking about?"

"There, read it for yourself." Holroyd pointed to a newspaper on his desk. Sean started reading while Holroyd poured himself a drink. Sean finished reading and looked at Holroyd.

"Is any of this true?"

"Some of the facts are correct," Holroyd admitted. "But there are facts that have been omitted, and much of the information from sources is nothing more than gossip. Perhaps some of that information is misinformation or is deliberately presented to lead to the conclusion everything is true," he added.

"Has mother seen this?"

"Yes."

"I bet she went batshit crazy."

"I think you understate her reaction," Holroyd remarked ruefully.

"What can we do?" asked Sean.

"For one, I won't be returning to Mexico in the near future to have another look at the stele. However, for the moment, you can do nothing other than try to find out who wrote that article about your project," Holroyd said. "I have to make some calls."

Chapter 50

Holroyd called Merry, and they agreed to meet over lunch at the Oxford and Cambridge Club on Pall Mall. Once lunch was over, they went into one of the smaller rooms to enjoy coffee and discuss events.

Holroyd gave an in-depth report on events in Mexico, including Li Feng's reminders to honour their agreement. He ended his report with a description of what Sean and his team had discovered, the publication of the article, and the attack on his son's team. Merry listened without interruption but then asked, "What about the article in the Canadian newspaper?"

"I'm not quite clear about that," Holroyd answered. "Some of the facts are correct, but the conclusions, even if only implied, are completely false. To be honest, I'm surprised the thing was even published." He paused. "I may have cause to sue for libel."

"The article claims reliable but anonymous sources for its facts," Merry pointed out. "Any idea who these sources might be?"

"No," Holroyd said. "But perhaps you would be in a better position to find out than I am."

"Perhaps." Merry thought for a moment. "Let's just get back to the players in Mexico. You mentioned you saw Li Feng and this fellow Strang at the massacre of the archeological team. What can you tell me about Strang?"

"He pretends to be an American government representative, and I think that is true. What I don't know for sure is which agency he belongs to and why he would know Li Feng or be present at the massacre." He stopped. "Unless he was in some sort of relationship with Li Feng. A relationship of which his agency is either aware and approves or is unaware and would be furious if they knew about it. "

"Any idea which it might be?"

"Not really," Holroyd answered. "But I believe he is very friendly with the local police chief. And that fellow gives me the willies." He stopped as the steward stopped by and refilled the coffee pot.

Once the man was out of earshot, Holroyd went on, "Philip told me that the chief is rumoured to have at least approved the murder of those policemen, including Jimenez."

"Philip?" asked Merry.

"Smythe-Jones Minor."

"Ah, yes." Merry thought for a moment. "Did you say this chief is somehow related to the de Perrefaltas?"

"I think so."

"Excellent," Merry exclaimed. "I think we've gone as far as we can now." He got out of his chair. "Keep in touch, will you?"

***

Holroyd was asleep when the phone rang. He tried to ignore it, but it continued to ring. Annoyed and still half asleep, he looked at the time. *Who is calling me at 2 a.m.? Must be a wrong number.* Finally, when the phone continued to ring, he picked it up. Before he could say anything, he heard Philip's voice.

"Peter!" Philip sounded excited. "You're not going to believe this."

"Damn it, Philip!" Holroyd grumbled. "Do you know what time it is?"

Philip was not about to be deterred. "I don't think you'll complain when I pass on the news."

"Well?" Holroyd mumbled, still wrestling between wakefulness and sleep.

"de Falta has resigned and left the country."

"Who?" Holroyd was still groggy.

"The local chief of police."

"What?" Holroyd was suddenly wide awake. "How did that come about?"

"The consul summoned his relative and, after pointing out that his activities and connections reflected badly on the family, suggested he resign."

"Just like that?" Holroyd was doubtful.

"He was also told that Strang had been put under investigation by some internal police force and could be arrested for his criminal involvement in the drugs trade. He would probably be offered some deal if he testified about all his activities and about others who worked with him. de Falta's name would most certainly top that list." Philip stopped.

In a more thoughtful tone, Philip went on, "Of course, while de Falta would never be able to work in Mexico again, he might escape a prison term if he were outside the country, such as visiting the family estates in Spain."

"And he accepted?"

"Manuel drove him to the airport a couple of hours ago."

"So, he's safe," Holroyd remarked. "That's a travesty of justice."

"I don't think so," Philip observed. "He could still be extradited for his complicity in the deaths of the policemen."

"Justice delayed is justice denied." Holroyd was bitter.

"Don't be so pessimistic," laughed Philip. "All the time he's basking on the estates, he'll be looking over his shoulder, wondering when retribution will arrive. I can't help but feel that's a punishment in and of itself."

"I just hope you're right," Holroyd observed. "But I must agree it's a step in the right direction." He thanked Philip, hung up, and tried to get back to sleep.

Chapter 51

Holroyd's phone rang again, and he recognised it was Pearl calling from China. He accepted the call, dreading what she was going to say. Before he could even say hello, she launched her attack.

"I have just spoken to my son," she spoke in a quiet but menacing tone that he knew better than he might have wished. "He has told me of the attack on him and his friends."

Holroyd's heart sank. "But he is alright...." He tried to rescue what he sensed might be a looming disaster.

"Don't interrupt me," she continued as if he had not spoken. "I warned you against getting into danger, but you did not obey me. I might have forgiven you for that, but now my son is also in danger, and I will not forgive that."

"But darling..."

"Again, you do not listen," her voice rose. "I told you not to interrupt me." She waited to let Holroyd consider just how fragile any defence might be. He decided discretion demanded he kept quiet until he could sense an opening.

"I will be coming home soon," Pearl continued, "and when I do, we will discuss what the future holds."

She hung up, leaving Holroyd in complete dis-
array. *Strewth, this time, I'm really in the doghouse.
God knows how I'm going to get out of it. And Sean
didn't help by running to her to tell her of his misfor-
tunes. I need to sit down with him very soon and explain the meaning of family solidarity. Perhaps together, we might be able to avert a complete family
disaster.*

Chapter 52

"Mickie, come in here, please," Breckenridge ordered peremptorily. Wondering what could possibly cause him to use such a tone, Mickie went to his office.

"Shut the door." Breckenridge did not seem to be in a happy mood. "I just got a call from the owner." He stopped to let her consider what this might mean. "Are you satisfied with your article? I mean are you absolutely sure of your sources?"

"Yes," Mickie said. "Why?"

"He received a legal letter requiring him to publish a retraction and to issue an apology."

"From whom?" she started. "Oh, wait! I bet it's from Holroyd."

"If that were so, I doubt he would have reacted in the way he did," Breckenridge remarked. "After all, such demands are not unusual in our business. Normally, we handle such matters with our legal counsel and do business as usual. But apparently, that's not the case here."

"Why?" asked Mickie. "What makes this matter so different?"

"For one, this matter has been launched individually by the American, British,   Mexican,   and

Spanish governments. The basic grounds are similar, and all deal with drug enforcement out of Mexico. I called in a few favours to see what else is going on."

Mickie waited.

"Did you know that this fellow Strang, whom you referred to me to corroborate your story, has been arrested? He faces multiple charges that include involvement in the drug trade, murder, kidnapping, and torture."

"What?" Mickie swayed as if she'd been pole-axed.

"Furthermore, "Breckenridge continued remorselessly, "the local chief of police is also charged and faces extradition back to Mexico or, more likely, to the States."

"How is that possible?" Mickie was aghast. "Why are the Americans involved in murder charges?"

"Several of the archeological team were Americans," Breckenridge reminded her. Mickie said nothing.

"Given what we have learned about your sources, you might want to think if you still want to stand by your article." Breckenridge stopped and waited for Mickie to say something. When she said nothing, he dismissed her with the instruction to prepare a written defence that he wanted on his desk by the end of the day.

After Mickie left, Breckenridge called the owner. "I think we're going to have to retract the article, issue an apology, and offer to discuss compensation."

Predictably, Simon O'Mallory was not pleased, and Breckenridge wondered if his newspaper days were about to end ignominiously.

The retraction and apology appeared in the next edition. Breckenridge looked over it again. *At least that exonerates Holroyd, and he might be able to continue his life and pursuits. He could now follow up on this Mexican stele business. Perhaps there will be a story there that we can publish and make amends for the damage done by Mickie's article.*

He regretted that the paper's lawyers had forbidden any mention of compensation.

Chapter 53

Merry wondered with which devil he had made a pact. Cheng had proven he would enforce their agreement without scruple and in a manner that would cause Merry the most harm. On the other hand, he had agreed to continue in his pursuit of drug suppliers based on promises the government had made but which promises he doubted they could fulfill. In either case, Song had to be taken out of his immediate care, and he felt a loss that he had never experienced before.

Furthermore, he worried about Holroyd's and Sean's safety, and the rescue of Rajeesh. *What was that abduction all about? Was that a message aimed at Peter, or was something else behind it?*

Finally, adding to his woes, his mother was after him to get married and produce an heir. Their last meeting had not been a pleasure.

"Meredith," his mother had started. "You have to get married and produce an heir. If you do not do so, the title and the estate will go to that useless cousin in Australia, and we both know that would be a disaster."

"Yes, mother," Merry had replied. "I'm fully aware of that, but I have Song to consider."

"What's to consider?" his mother had asked. "I know you have strong feelings for him, and I will admit he is a delightful man. But you must not let your feelings override your duties. And anyway, find yourself and marry a broodmare who can produce an heir and then keep her while you lavish your feelings on Song." She looked sternly at him before continuing. "Just don't make a fuss about your arrangements."

"Just keep out of it, mother." Merry had tried to change the subject, but his mother was not put off quite so easily.

"You wouldn't be the first member of the family to have, shall we say, unconventional family arrangements. The seventh Duke, your great-great-grandfather, maintained quite a stable of pretty young things of both sexes." She stopped and then, with a smile, went on. "We're never sure if someone is related to us."

"Alright, then," Merry said, exasperated by his mother's insistence. "Go out and find a broodmare, and when you have done so, I can decide what I will do.

"Yes, dear," his mother had said demurely, savouring her victory. Merry just stormed out the door, slamming it behind him. *What am I going to tell Song? And how will he react?*

Chapter 54

"Excuse this unannounced visit, Doctor Holroyd." Manorford stood at the door in the company of his Sergeant. "I wonder if you can help us, sir."

"Of course," Holroyd stood aside as they entered. Once seated, Holroyd asked, "What can I do for you, Inspector?"

"Have you received any communication about the abduction of the young man?"

"No," Holroyd answered. "And I'm not clear why I would."

"We were wondering if the abduction is related to your searches in Mexico," Manorford said. "If that were the case, I would have expected the kidnappers to have made some demands on you. If they haven't, perhaps the kidnapping has another purpose."

"I see your point," Holroyd replied. "But if there is another purpose, I don't know what it might be."

"Just how annoyed were you when you discovered that published article?" asked Manorford.

"What has that to do with the abduction?" Holroyd asked.

"Humour me, sir," Manorford insisted.

Holroyd hesitated before replying. "I was annoyed that someone had betrayed my trust by publishing without my prior approval. But I think whoever it may have been might have exposed me, the others on his team, and himself to danger."

"And you have no idea who that person might be?"

"No."

"But you have suspicions?"

"Yes," Holroyd answered. "Probably someone on my son's team or someone who worked closely with the team."

"That certainly seems likely," Manorford observed. "And just what sort of danger might that be, sir?"

"Inspector, whenever you broadcast you know where there is buried treasure all sorts of people become interested," Holroyd observed. "And not all of those people are very nice in how they go about asking for the information."

"And are you aware of any such people?"

"Not directly," Holroyd lied.

"Not directly?" Manorford echoed. "But indirectly, sir? Would you care to give me the names of whom you suspect?"

"Not yet, Inspector," Holroyd said, "I don't want to send you on a wild goose chase."

"That's very considerate of you, sir," Manorford looked intensely at Holroyd. "But it's up to us to decide if it's a goose chase." He paused to let Holroyd think about that before asking, "But you wouldn't be a person to send us on such a chase, would you, sir?"

"Inspector," Holroyd infuriated, glared at the Inspector, his voice rising. "That's a preposterous suggestion." He calmed down to continue in an icy voice. "How did you get that idea?"

"We interviewed the young man who's still in hospital," Manorford replied.

"And what did you learn from him?" asked Holroyd.

"He thought you were reluctant to have the police asking questions, and he wondered why."

Holroyd was speechless.

"Thank you for your help, sir," Manorford said. "We will be getting back to you." And the policemen took their leave.

Holroyd sat back to consider what had just transpired. All else aside, he realised he was now under suspicion for the abduction. *Not again! Why is it that every time I'm doing my research, I somehow end up as a suspect in a murder or an abduction? I think I had better have a serious talk with Sean to find out what he hasn't told me.* But his heart sank at the prospect of interrogating his son for a possible crime. Reluctantly, he called Sean, but there was no answer, and he left a message.

While waiting for Sean to get in touch, he poured himself a stiff drink and tried to think the situation through. *Is Li Feng behind this? I wouldn't put it past him. If he is, I can expect a call soon enough; until then, I must wait.*

He poured himself another drink. *Pearl will love this! She'll probably come home accompanied by a divorce lawyer. And Wen Mei Li will probably add me to her most wanted list and post a reward for my head on a platter. These are not exactly comforting prospects.*

Chapter 55

Predictably, Song was not happy.

"Why Merry?" he wailed. "Why must you marry? Don't you love me enough?"

"Of course I love you," Merry took a deep breath. "But I have to consider that I need a son to carry the family name and to inherit the title and the estate. Unfortunately, you cannot do that for me."

"Can't I have a sex change?" Song asked hopefully. "Wouldn't that work?"

"I don't think that would work." Merry sounded regretful. "Much as I wish it would."

"So we have to separate?" Song was close to tears.

"Perhaps," Merry said, "But perhaps not."

"What do you mean?"

"We could stay together if my wife accepts you as my lover," Merry answered.

"Is that possible?" Song sounded doubtful.

"Oh, I wouldn't be the first British aristocrat to have a wife and a lover at the same time. Though I admit, I've never heard of a case where the wife and the lover were of different sexes." He lingered. "Probably because such cases were never discussed outside the immediate family."

"You mean if we can find you a wife who will give you a son," Song said, "we can still be together?"

"Yes."

"Then I will ask my family to find you a suitable wife," Song said happily. "One who will give you many sons and who will also be happy that I am with you."

Merry was mulling over his probable loss of Song and answered distractedly, "That sounds like a really good idea."

Chapter 56

"Doctor Holroyd," Li Feng's voice came down the line. "Once again, you have disappointed me."

"You can hardly expect to keep my word when you don't keep yours," Holroyd riposted with more bravado than he really felt.

"You surprise me," Li Feng said. "I am unaware that I failed to live up to our agreement. But Perhaps you will be so good as to enlighten me."

"You have attacked my son." Holroyd's voice rose. "And that is unforgivable."

"Your son?" asked Li Feng. "Why would I be interested in your son?"

"Li Feng, please don't treat me like a fool," Holroyd replied. "We both know why."

"I assure you; I have no idea."

Holroyd was taken aback. *Li Feng has never lied outright to me. Could he be telling the truth?* He tried to find out and shot back, "I suppose you will tell me you did not read the article detailing his deciphering the writing on the stele."

"No," Li Feng said, "but since you have raised the subject, I will make sure I do, and when I have done so, you and I will discuss just why you did not pass the information on to me as we had agreed."

"If you have not read the article, why did you attack my son?" Holroyd insisted.

"Did you fail to hear me tell you I have no knowledge of an attack on your son?"

"Have it your way then," Holroyd retorted but went on to describe the attack and the abduction of Rajeesh.

"It was pure luck my son was not hurt or taken."

Li Feng was silent and then said, "Doctor Holroyd, I had nothing to do with that. Now I will find this article and be assured we will talk again."

The call ended. *Good luck with finding the article, Li Feng. I doubt you or any of your henchmen subscribe to that website, and without the proper keywords, you won't have much luck even finding it.*

***

Holroyd went out to do grocery shopping but on passing a newsvendor noted the headlines in the local newspaper announcing the abduction. He bought the paper and started reading.

Shorn of all the rhetoric about terrorism and the rise of crime, the article was accurate. He noted that Sean's name was there and a reference to himself as a noted professor engaged in hunting for ancient Chinese treasures. *This implies I had a hand in the abduction. It's all I need! I'm a dead duck if Pearl reads this before I can talk to her.*

He tried to call Sean again, but again there was no answer, and he left a message that they should meet as soon as possible. He changed his intention to shop and went home. He was hanging up his coat when Sean arrived.

"We need to talk," Holroyd opened the conversation. "What do you really know about the publication of your article?"

"Nothing that I haven't already told you," Sean answered, but Holroyd sensed a defensiveness that he couldn't remember ever having sensed before.

"Sean," Holroyd insisted, "this is becoming very serious."

"What do you mean?" Sean asked, but again, Holroyd sensed Sean was not open.

"Come on, Sean." Holroyd showed his impatience by raising his voice and adopting an abrupt tone. "There was that attack on you and your team. Rajeesh has been abducted, and to put the icing on the cake, some very nasty people have become aware of the article. So don't evade my questions."

"What nasty people, and why would they be interested?" Sean was still avoiding the main question.

"We can discuss that later," Holroyd said. "Right now, who wrote the article, and why was it published?"

"Father, I don't know," Sean said.

"Then why do the police think I might have arranged the attack as a revenge for one of you for its publication?" Holroyd demanded.

"Why would they think that?" Sean showed a sudden interest.

"Because they interviewed Viktor, and he suggested that."

"But that's not what happened," Sean blurted out.

"Oh?" Holroyd asked. "So you know what happened?" Sean remained silent. "I think now would be a good time to tell me everything before matters get completely out of control."

"I've told you everything I know." Sean was becoming truculent and left the room. Next, Holroyd heard the front door close.

Holroyd was stunned. *Where is he off to now? Why is he so defensive? Does he know what happened? Did he, or all three of them, plan the whole thing without realising what the consequences might be? This is a side of him that I didn't know about. Suddenly, I don't know my own son!!!*

Chapter 57

Holroyd's phone rang as he waited for Sean to return, and he answered without first checking to see who the caller might be.

"So, have you come to your senses and tell me what's happening?" he asked brusquely.

"I say, that's not very sporting of you," Merry answered. "Care to explain that?"

"Merry?" Holroyd was caught unawares. "I'm sorry, I thought you were someone else calling."

"I feel sorry for whoever that someone might be," Merry remarked.

"Look, I'm waiting for an important call," Holroyd snapped. "Can this call wait?"

"As you wish," Merry answered. "I'll call back when it's convenient."

"No! wait!" Holroyd calmed down. "Since you're on the line, I have a suggestion for catching Li Feng."

"Go on," Merry said, interested.

"I want to persuade him to return to the stele, and you to arrange to have a reception committee ready for him when he arrives."

"Go on," Merry observed. "But we need something to make him think it would be worth his while." He paused to let Holroyd think about the idea.

"That article about my son's work would probably do the trick," Holroyd said. "Li Feng knows about it, but without the passwords, I don't think he'll be able to get at it very soon."

"Oh! You think that article is good enough?" Merry asked. "My people didn't think much of it."

"How on earth….?" Holroyd began.

"Come off it, Peter," Merry interrupted. "You know I have many sources of information, and one of them let me know why the local police are investigating the abduction of Sean's teammate."

He waited for Holroyd to comment. When Holroyd said nothing, Merry went on, "Well, so you think the article contains enough information to wet Li Feng's appetite."

"Yes," Holroyd said, "except I have no idea how to get in touch with him. He calls me."

"Then let's hope he does so soon," Merry observed. "When he does so, let us know, will you?" and hung up.

The call came sooner than Holroyd expected.

"Once again, Doctor Holroyd," Li Feng said. "You dare to play games with me."

"Really?" Holroyd feigned ignorance. "How so, this time?"

"As you probably knew all along," Li Feng said. "I could not retrieve the article you implied I should read."

"Oh, I am so sorry." Holroyd assumed as contrite a tone as he could. "Then let me make amends. But I shall require your assurance you will leave my family alone."

"I will make no such promise," Li Feng replied angrily. "However, I will promise to concern myself with their well-being should you fail yet again to meet my demand."

Holroyd remained silent to give Li Feng the impression that he was deliberating on what to do. Finally, resignedly, "It seems I have little choice. Give me an address, and I will pass over the access details."

The call ended, and Holroyd did as he had promised. Once that was done, he called Merry to let him know Li Feng had been given the information.

"Thanks, Peter," Merry said, "I think Wen Mei Li might want her forces at the mine to be the reception committee. I'll have to call her."

Wen Mei Li thought it was a good suggestion.

Chapter 58

"Thank goodness you've come to your senses." Merry's mother welcomed him into the sitting room. "You've had fun, but now you must settle down, produce an heir, and attend to the estate."

"Yes, mother," Merry answered. "But let's not count our chickens just yet. You promised to find me a suitable wife, and so far, I've not met any potentially suitable duchesses."

"Don't worry about that." His mother grinned. "I've invited several families to bring their available womenfolk for a weekend visit. I'm hoping at least one nubile lady will attract your attention." She stopped. "Despite your preferences, which we will not discuss, you will do your duty."

"Yes, mother." Merry sighed and went into his study. He opened his emails and noted one from a sender he did not recognise but appeared to have a Thai name. Curious about what it might be, he opened it to find an album of photographs of young Thai ladies.

"Damn dating sites," he remarked. "Don't know how they got my address." He was about to delete it when he noticed the name Song in the text. The sender reported that Song had asked the family to suggest a possible wife and the photographs of some he might consider. "How very timely," he mused and, after an initial look, downloaded the pictures for examination after the household had retired for the night.

After dinner and wishing his mother good night, Merry returned to his computer and examined the pictures he had been sent. Two aroused some interest: one resembling Song, and the other had a beautiful face with an alluring smile that Merry found hard to resist. He sent a message requesting more information about those two before bed.

The next morning, he found a reply and, after careful consideration, asked that they both come to London for a meeting. He promised to fund their travel and gave instructions on obtaining tickets and visitor's visas.

Chapter 59

Holroyd heard the front door open and waited for Sean to come in. When he did so, Holroyd was surprised that Rajeesh was also there. He looked at the two youths.

"Would one of you explain this?" he finally asked.

Sean looked at Rajeesh and said, "I think you had better do so."

Rajeesh said nothing but looked at the carpet, embarrassed.

"Well?" Holroyd asked.

Rajeesh mumbled something.

"Speak up," Holroyd commanded, but Rajeesh said nothing.

"Sean, can you help your friend?" Holroyd asked impatiently, "It appears the cat got his tongue."

"It was supposed to be a joke," Sean muttered. "We never thought it would cause any harm."

"Well, it has," retorted Holroyd. "So exactly what did you do?"

Sean looked at Rajeesh. "Will you tell him?"

Rajeesh shook his head, still looking at the carpet. Sean sighed.

"His parents were hounding Rajeesh to show that he had honoured their trust in sending him here. They wanted tangible proof to show for all the support they had given him."

"And?" asked Holroyd.

"So we wrote the article to show them."

"We?" echoed Holroyd. "So you were involved also?"

"Yes," admitted Sean.

"And then what happened?"

"His parents didn't believe it was important and accused him of fabricating something to impress them."

"Go on." Holroyd was not liking what he was hearing but realised he had to have the full story.

"We organized a fake kidnap to give the impression it was important enough for someone to kidnap Rajeesh to get the information out of him."

"Is Viktor also in on this?" Holroyd asked.

"Yes," admitted Sean.

"Of all the asinine escapades I've heard, this has to top the list. Have you any idea how much trouble you've caused?" Holroyd asked. "For one, Viktor ended up in hospital due to this 'supposed to be a joke.' And all three of you could be charged with wasting police time by your stupid stunt. And the police probably have a few more charges ready." He stopped. "Right. You will all write a confession and letters of apology to Rajeesh's parents, the University, and the police. As for your futures, let's hope this will not harm your prospects. Are we clear?"

Both nodded.

"Not one word to your mother, Sean," Holroyd commanded. "Ever."

Sean nodded.

"Both of you, out!" Holroyd waved at them. "Start writing now."

Chapter 60

"I'm off to the office," Merry told his mother, "And I'll be up in London for most of the week. You can always get me at the office or the club."

"That's fine," his mother responded. "I'll be setting up the social weekend while you're away. So be prepared when you return."

After arranging his stay at his club, Merry phoned his office to arrange a meeting to catch up on where matters stood. That being done, he called the Ritz to enquire if his guests had arrived. On learning that they had arrived the day before, he asked they be told he would be coming over later that day.

His arrival was greeted by the assistant manager and escorted to the suite where the guests were staying. Before he entered, he ordered that Thai tea, coffee, and biscuits be brought up.

On entering, he was met by an older man and two Thai women. Over the next two hours, he learned one was Song's cousin, who spoke no English, and the other was the man's daughter, who also acted as the translator for the trio.

Song's cousin strongly resembled Song, and Merry felt a sudden warm flush as he looked at her. Her name was Hathai. The translator's name was Ambhon, and Merry felt drawn to her as he had never been drawn to a woman before. But he was in no hurry to decide whether he wanted to develop further relationships with either.

He welcomed them to England and explained that he had business to attend to, but they should amuse themselves. They could visit places of interest, and he would arrange for a Thai-speaking guide. They could also shop and charge their purchases to the account here at the hotel. He would join them for dinner and in the evenings. Later, he invited them to come down to his estate.

Satisfied with his arrangements, he took his leave.

Chapter 61

"**W**ell, Peter," Merry answered Holroyd's call, "what can I do for you today?"

"I've solved the abduction," Holroyd said, relating his conversation with the boys.

"Boys will be boys," was all Merry said. "But I agree that was probably out of bounds. I'll make a few calls and see if we can't persuade the constabulary to let them off with a stern warning. But do try to make sure they don't do anything quite like that again."

Holroyd thanked him.

"And to bring you up to date," Merry said, "Our trap for Li Feng is baited and set. All we can do is wait and see if he will spring it."

***

"Have you decided on your bride?" Merry's mother asked.

"Yes, I have."

"Excellent," his mother almost purred with satisfaction. "And who is to be the future Duchess?"

"Ambhon."

"What?" His mother sat up. "That Thai girl? Have you lost your senses?"

"Not at all."

"She will never be accepted into society," his mother protested. "And your son will be a half-caste. That won't sit well in the House of Lords."

"Wake up, Mother," Merry said calmly. "Times have changed. Today, so-called mixed marriages are quite normal and produce beautiful, healthy children. Look at Peter Holroyd and his Chinese wife, and I can think of a few aristocrats who adopted a ménage-à-trois and were still accepted in society."

"Ménage-à-trois?" His mother's face sagged.

"Song will continue to be part of the household."

"I see." His mother slowly sank back into her chair.

Merry looked at her. *That went better than I had expected, and I think she'll come around. Thank goodness, she and Song formed a bond that might help smooth things quickly.*

***

"I see you managed to decipher the stele and that there is treasure there, even if the precise location is not revealed," Li Feng opened the telephone conversation, "But do not think of retrieving it. You might find you are not welcome in Mexico."

"I suppose you will spare me the necessity of trying," Holroyd remarked, "but what you fail to understand is that I have met my objective by finding the stele and its inscription. It never was about treasure. On the other hand, you might not succeed if you go there yourself." And he hung up.

The next call was not long in coming.

"Did you really think to trap me with armed men waiting at the stele?" Li Feng left a voicemail message. "I was warned not to go there. But there will be a time when it will be convenient. In the meantime, again, you underestimate me, and how I will reward your failure to cooperate. I will be in touch."

***

Holroyd called Merry to inform him of Li Feng's call.

"Not to worry, old boy," Merry said, "I'm sure there will be another occasion. But while we're talking, you are invited to my wedding."

"Your wedding?" Holroyd asked, surprised, "What brought that on?"

Merry explained how he had been persuaded and mentioned that it would be a menage-à-trois.

"Say that again?" Holroyd asked. Merry did so, and Holroyd remained silent for a moment before saying, "Well done. I suspected your preferences, but to be honest, I never thought you'd come right out like this. I'm delighted for you."

Chapter 62

"Mother is arriving this afternoon," Sean announced, "and asked me to pick her up at the airport." He hesitated before continuing. "She said you are not to come."

"Probably for the best," Holroyd admitted. "I think I'm not in her good books right now." Sean just nodded and left to go to the airport. Holroyd waited at home, worried as to what would happen next.

He was unable to distract himself from his family's worries. He thought of going out for a walk or maybe a drink at the local pub but decided he'd better be at home when Sean returned. As a result, he was left wandering aimlessly around the flat.

When Sean returned, Holroyd was surprised to see he was accompanied by Pearl, who approached, hugged, and kissed him.

"I am so happy to be back," she said. "And you are safe. But we still have things to talk about." And with that, she went to her room to unpack

Holroyd looked at Sean.

"What happened to your mother?" he asked. "I thought I was about to be hung, drawn, and quartered when she got back."

"You were," laughed Sean. "However, she was given a newspaper on the plane. In it, she read a complete retraction of the article accusing you of being in the drug trade. They even apologised."

"Thank goodness," said Holroyd, relieved. "So all is peace and quiet again."

"Not quite." Pearl reappeared from her room. "You have been cleared of all those nasty accusations but not of putting our son in danger." She waved a copy of the local newspaper. "This says you planned it."

"Where did you get that?" Holroyd asked, horrified..

"Lying on the floor in the bathroom." She looked at the menfolk. "Perhaps one of you left it there for me to find."

Sean suddenly left the room.

"Oh," was all Holroyd could muster.

Disclaimer

All persons named in this book, except for historical or publicly known individuals, are fictitious and in no way intended to reflect any living or dead person.

Acknowledgements

The author wishes to acknowledge the invaluable help of Lizy J Campbell, Lydia Gionet, Paul Morisset, and Richard Odey.

About the Author

Peter King was born in Scotland and grew up in Switzerland and England before coming to Canada to study civil engineering at McGill University. He obtained his MBA at Western University and his doctorate from the University of Phoenix at age seventy. He  spent his career as a naval officer, a public servant, a consultant to First Nations, and a professor at the University of Hearst. For fifteen years, he was a professor at the Beijing University of Technology. He has competed and coached in fencing, rowing, and cross-country skiing. He was also an international umpire refereeing at the world rowing championships. He has been recognized by federal, provincial, and municipal governments in Canada and by the City of Beijing in China. He has published mystery novels, a poetry book, a history of rowing, and several academic papers.